"Do you plan to be my sweet persuader?"

Rique's question was sarcastic.

"I plan to persuade you to rejoin the human race," Angie agreed, "but you don't make me feel very sweet about the prospect. I don't relish the idea of being your nurse, Rique. You were always rather arrogant and sure of yourself."

"And now I've been taken down a peg or two, eh?" His hands shot out and instinctively found her, jerking her to him. Angie didn't struggle; she couldn't—she'd never been more aware of him as a man.

"Did you imagine I'd be easy to handle because I'm blind?" he asked.

"Did you imagine, Rique, that blindness would make you less of a man?"

A quiver seemed to go through him. "Don't go probing into my thoughts and feelings, Angie—you might discover things you won't like!"

VIOLET WINSPEAR
is also the author of these

Harlequin Presents

and these
Harlequin Romances

Many of these titles are available at your local bookseller.

For a free catalogue listing all available Harlequin Romances
and Harlequin Presents, send your name and address to:

HARLEQUIN READER SERVICE,
M.P.O. Box 707, Niagara Falls, NY 14302
Canadian address: Stratford, Ontario N5A 6W2

VIOLET WINSPEAR

love's agony

Harlequin Books

TORONTO • LONDON • LOS ANGELES • AMSTERDAM
SYDNEY • HAMBURG • PARIS • STOCKHOLM • ATHENS • TOKYO

Harlequin Presents edition published August 1981
ISBN 0-373-10450-2

Original hardcover edition published in 1981
by Mills & Boon Limited

CHAPTER ONE

As the launch drew closer to the island of Bayaltar the shape of it could be seen, a great altar-like rock rising out of the blue Mediterranean.

Upon the island lived a colony of people of mixed nationality, foremost among them the affluent Spaniards who had built houses among the tall tropical trees and were very much in command of the island's welfare and commerce.

Angie sat there in the launch and felt her heart throbbing with a mixture of emotions. Six years ago she had bade goodbye to Bayaltar, and today she returned, no longer a schoolgirl of sixteen but a young woman in whose luggage was folded the uniform of a dedicated, first-rate nurse who had a formidable task awaiting her at the residence of Carlos de Zaldo, the Governor-General of the island.

The launch swung in an arc towards the landing jetty and the sunlight on the sea made it sparkle vividly. A sigh of pure nostalgia caught Angie by the throat; even the trepidation that she felt couldn't lessen the sense of enchantment which she had always felt for Bayaltar and which the years in between hadn't dimmed. It might have been only yesterday when she used to come and spend part of the summer and winter holidays with the Governor's family.

Maya de Zaldo had attended the same school as Angie in England and it was there that the two girls had become close friends. Angie had no family of her own after her Aunt Kit died and she had thought it so kind and generous of Maya's family to invite her to stay with them. Right away she had liked them and found their big Spanish house the most fascinating place on earth. They were very affluent members of the island's aristocracy and with quite a range of power. Don Carlos was the very epitome of the Latin *hidalgo*, and he and his children enjoyed a grand style of living far removed from what Angie had known with her aunt. Angie was fortunate enough to attend the Convent of the Holy Virgin owing to an endowment settled upon her when she was born. She learned only after her 'aunt's' death that they had really been mother and daughter.

Who her father had been and if he was still alive somewhere in England remained a mystery Angie had never attempted to solve. Her beloved 'Aunt Kit' was gone and Angie wanted her to rest in peace. If it had been her choice never to speak of the love affair which had resulted in a child whom Kitty Hart had chosen to call her niece rather than her daughter, then Angie respected her wishes. They had been poor, but the affection between them had been lavish and it had left Angie with memories which she cherished.

Her memories of Bayaltar were shot through with more disturbing emotions, reawakened last week when Maya had reached her by telephone and told her that Rique de Zaldo had been badly wounded during a mission into the Basque country; now he was at home and in need of a nurse.

'Tell me,' Angie's fingers had crushed themselves against the handset of the telephone, 'everything!'

'It's dreadful!' Maya had said it with a desperate

note in her voice. 'Fragments of the bomb struck him in the face and head and—oh, Angie, poor Rique can't see—he's blind!'

Angie gazed blindly at the upflung water as the launch drew in against the jetty wall. How well remembered were those eyes of Rique's. She had realised during that last holiday at his father's house that she would never again meet anyone who would walk into her heart as if it were a room awaiting his sole occupation.

Six years and Angie could feel each anxious beat of her heart as her taxi-cab drove along the Ramblas de las Virtudes which ran in almost a straight line from the big open plaza where on Saturday evenings a military band played and groups of people sat at the café tables and enjoyed conversation and coffee. Along the main street were all sorts of shops and bazaars, and she and Maya had often wandered there and no shadows had spoiled the warm sunlight. There had been no warning that when she came again to Bayaltar she would come with a heart that ached.

As the cab drew nearer all the time to the Residencia, so eye-catching where it stood upon the cliffs that towered above the island, she wondered if there would be a change in her innermost feelings when she saw Rique again. Even in the midst of her busy hospital work she had often thought about him, far away in Spain where he had been serving with the army for as long as she had been serving as a nurse.

The cab turned on to the road that wended upwards towards the Casera de Nusta where shaggy, thick-stemmed palm trees caught the sun through their long leaves. This was the winding Street of Saints, leading past the sunken garden of the Cemetery and the

Spanish Chapel whose bells echoed across the water.
The rambling roadside walls were cloaked in mignon-
ette, jasmine and clumps of mimosa that would scent
the air when the sun declined, spreading its dazzling
gold and flame across the sea.

Love of the island had seeded itself in Angie's heart
just as love for the Governor's eldest son had grown
secretly within her. No one knew of it . . . Rique least
of all.

Within an hour of Maya de Zaldo's telephone call
Angie had arranged through the nursing agency to be
sent to Bayaltar so she could take care of the man she
had found so unforgettable. She was quite certain
Rique knew nothing of her feelings; as a teenager she
had been rather shy of him and constrained in his
company. Already he had seemed adult and slightly
aloof in the way of the Latin *señorito*.

The children of Carlos de Zaldo were constantly
aware of their father's importance on the island, but
Angie had never found them too proud. It had seemed
natural of Rique de Zaldo to be rather haughty . . .
someone individual and darkly romantic, his air of
aloofness intensified by blade-grey eyes that somehow
shielded him from entry into his thoughts.

Riveting eyes, so in contrast to his raven hair and
straight black brows . . . and how well he had walked,
with the grace and control of a swordsman, Angie had
always thought. She couldn't bear to think of him as
blind and stumbling . . . everything within her cried
out against such an image; not Rique who had been so
vital, so assured, so charged with force and courage
and the need to make use of his energies.

Suddenly Angie tensed as the Residencia came into
view, with its gleaming white walls, horseshoe arches

and tall watchtower where a guard was always on duty.

She gazed spellbound at the house as the cab drove in under the entrance arch and came to a stop as another of the Governor's guards stepped from the doorway of the gatehouse and demanded to know their business. Angie leaned from the cab and quietly mentioned her name; at once there was a change in the man's attitude and they were allowed to proceed towards the front entrance of the great house that merged so well with the adamantine rock and clambering plants. The patio was cloistered and behind iron-grilled balconies were windows set deep in emblazoned glass. It had a secretive air, like something out of a Grimms' tale of witches and spells.

For Angie not a fraction of the old magic had diminished, and as she stood there on the patio she recalled the games they had played up there in the watchtower with its winding stairs. One of her favourite places in this wonderful warren of a house was the garden room where a fountain splashed into a green marble pool where chiffon-tailed fish swam round and round, and where there were high-backed cane chairs and a cool and quiet atmosphere.

The cab drove away and Angie let her gaze drift around the patio; she needed a few minutes alone in which to gather her composure and to brace herself for the moment when she came face to face with Rique, not only as his nurse but as a woman who cared for him. It wasn't going to be easy, for instead of the assured army officer she was going to confront a man whose career was at an end; whose sight had been blasted into darkness.

'Are the doctors absolutely sure about his . . .

blindness?' she had asked Maya. 'The optic nerves could still be intact and given time and care——'

'They told Papa not to expect any miracles——' Maya had broken down at the phone and the sound of her weeping had brought the tears heavy and hot into Angie's eyes. 'Oh, Angie, I can hardly bear to look at him!'

'Don't tell me——'

'He's been hurt all down one side of his face. They're going to skin-graft later on and they insist he won't look unsightly, but it breaks my heart to see him like that! What did Rique ever do to deserve it?'

A bird called across the patio and the sun was filling the sky with a flush of scarlet.

Angie stirred out of her sad thoughts, someone called her name and there was Maya running from the house to greet her. 'Thank God you came!' They hugged each other, there beneath the looming balconies of the house where they had laughed and sung and every day had seemed like summer.

'How is he?' Angie breathed.

'So ... changed,' Maya sighed. 'So brooding and sarcastic, letting no one near him. Most of the time he sits by himself in the garden room and stares into the fountain pool as if he can see the fish, and it's as if his thoughts go round and round, never giving him a moment's rest. At night I hear him stumbling about— he hasn't yet accustomed himself to the house and several times he has fallen over, but if anyone tries to help him, he snarls and says something hurtful. The good God knows he was so sure and certain in every way— you remember the way he was, don't you, Angie?'

Angie remembered vividly and fought back the tears

that burned in her eyes. 'Has Rique,' she swallowed the lump in her throat, 'has he been told that I'm to be his nurse?'

Maya nodded, but the reddening sunlight on her face showed that she was biting her lip.

'He doesn't like the idea, does he?' Angie was unsurprised. Rique had his Latin pride and it would infuriate him, his need to be helped to overcome the handicap of being blind . . . someone who must watch him closely for any sign that his injury wasn't causing ominous complications. His doctor would supply her with the medical details of the case, but her training as a nurse forewarned her that head wounds could be unpredictable, especially when the victim had been hurt by the fragmentation of a bomb.

Angie lifted her suitcase and walked with Maya into the Residencia whose look and smell were blessedly unchanged. She took a deep breath of the beeswax polish that gave the mahogany furniture its lustre, bringing out the detail of the crisp Spanish carving. Mingling with the smell of polish she caught the whiff of a *cigarillo*, those slender dark cigarettes that Spaniards liked to smoke.

'It could have been yesterday that I was here,' she said huskily.

'Why did you stay away from us?' Maya gripped her hand. 'You weren't always so busy that you couldn't pay us a visit.'

'You'd be amazed how hard a nurse does work.' Angie's smile was strained . . . it was because of Rique she had stayed away, and now because of Rique she had returned.

She and his sister stood beneath the big chandeliers

on brass chains and set against the white walls of the
hall were big carved chairs and cabinets into which
patterns in pearl and silver had been interwoven.
Across the floor were immense Oriental rugs, lending
rich colour to the dark dignity of the furnishings.

The surroundings very much suited Maya de Zaldo,
with her dark hair drawn back into a smooth knot to
reveal her large amber eyes and Latin-boned face.
Angie's fairness of hair was in striking contrast, a
frame for a face that was vital rather than pretty.

Amber eyes looked into Angie's grey-blue ones,
searchingly. 'You look so grown up, Angie, so *right* as
a nurse. I can't tell you how glad I am that you
came—perhaps Rique will let you help him.'

'I'm going to insist on it.' Angie summoned a smile
in an effort to dispel her friend's anxiety. 'I've learned
how to be firm with obstinate patients.'

'Strange that you became a nurse,' Maya said
thoughtfully. 'Father has always been fond of you—I
believe you remind him of our mother because of your
colouring. She was that rarity, a Latin woman with
fair skin and hair, and of course the grey eyes that
Rique inherited.'

'I remember the portrait of your mother in the
salita. She was much prettier than me.'

'I always wanted to have hair like yours, Angie.
Why did you have those lovely thick plaits cut off?'

'Rique had a habit of pulling them.' Angie's smile
wavered. 'I prefer my hair this way, just clear of my
shoulders. It looks tidier with my nurse's cap.'

Angie glanced along the hall to where a range of
stained-glass windows caught the last rays of the dying
sun. 'I'm glad this house is still the same, nothing
about it seems to have changed.'

'Only Rique has changed.' Maya's gaze dwelt upon the coloured windows of the garden room, and Angie felt her pulses quicken. Was he in there right now, sitting in one of the fan-backed chairs in the dusk, and was it the smoke of his *cigarillo* that drifted silently into the hall? How she yearned to see him again, and yet how she shrank from the moment when she must see his injured face and look into his blind eyes that would only remember her as a gawky schoolgirl.

'When shall I see Rique?' she asked. 'Has he been told that I'd be arriving today?'

Maya nodded. 'He doesn't join us at mealtimes, he's still so sensitive about being clumsy with his food and he eats alone in his sitting-room, and sometimes in the garden room. He's in there right now—you guessed as much, didn't you?'

'I can smell a *cigarillo*. Shall I go in and take the bull by the horns? He has to be faced sooner or later.'

Maya looked at Angie in amazement. 'Don't tell me you are nervous of Rique? You look calm enough.'

'I'm well trained, but my butterflies aren't.' Angie pressed a hand to her midriff. 'He could always intimidate me, and since last we met he's been a soldier and seen action. He's seen people die in awful ways and been a victim of violence himself. He's your brother Rique, yet at the same time he's a man I—I don't really know, and he's bound to resent me because I must nurse him and watch him——'

'Watch him?' Maya took her up.

'In case he stumbles over something,' Angie said hastily. It wouldn't do to let Maya know that it would be part of her job to watch for signs of any deterioration in Rique's general health and behaviour. Maya loved him and was already worried sick about him.

'You never thought to come back to Bayaltar on such a sad occasion, is that not so?' Maya's eyes were bleak.

'I would have wished for anything but this.' Angie couldn't keep a break out of her voice; seeing Rique again was going to hurt like hell and she prayed for enough composure to carry her through the next half hour. It was going to come as a shock seeing him blind and scarred because the person she remembered had only to enter a room and the atmosphere became charged with a vital excitement. The eyes she recalled had only to dwell upon a girl and her bones seemed to melt. To Rique she had been but a schoolgirl with plaits to pull, but to her he had been a man; tall, lean and dangerous in a way she understood now she was no longer an adolescent girl.

'Come and say hello to him.' Maya drew her in the direction of the garden room and the scent of *cigarillo* smoke grew stronger. As it stole through the partly open door it mingled with the scent of the various plants and flowers with which the room was generously stocked throughout the year. Herbs for the kitchen were grown here in pots, and as Angie breathed them a spate of memories swept over her.

The only source of light shone slumbrously from under the globe of a candlelamp. Cane creaked and a long pair of legs shifted as the man in the chair turned his head. The blind eyes searched, and in the shaded lamplight Angie saw the lean and wounded profile, the black hair shaved away at the temple where the surgeon had probed for the shell fragments.

As a nurse she had seen worse facial damage, but this was Rique, and as a woman she wanted to run to him, to wrap her arms about him and draw his head to her breast.

'*Quien es?*'

'It's I, Maya.'

'Who is with you?'

'Take a guess, *amigo mio.*' His sister walked to his chair and leaned down to lay a kiss against his scars. He pulled his head away sharply and Angie caught the glitter of his sightless eyes, undamaged to look at and still brilliantly pierced by those points of mica. She felt a sense of breathless relief that the bomb hadn't seared all the magnetism out of those eyes. Below his cheekbones there were hollows filled with shadow, and six years had added to that proud look of the Castilian whose ancestry reached back into the past.

'We meet again, Rique de Zaldo,' Angie said in Spanish, for long ago these people had polished her schoolgirl grammar and accent.

'Ah, so it's my little sister of mercy,' he rejoined, in sardonic English. 'As you can see, I have never been in better shape, blind as a bat in a cave and likely to go as mad as a hatter. *Bienvenida,* Angela.'

She walked to his chair and saw his hand seeking blindly the handle of the white stick that rested against the arm; his clumsy search sent it clattering to the floor and he cursed in Spanish.

'Don't stir.' She placed a hand gently on his shoulder. 'You look so comfortable in here, with the cool sound of the water splashing into the fish pool. It's such a relaxing place.'

'Quite.' He bit out the word. 'Now I'm an enfeebled wreck I need the relaxation; it might just stop me from hurling the furniture through the windows, always supposing I could locate them. Well, *mi niña*, and how are you these days? Enjoying the task of patting the pillows and smoothing the pained brows?'

'I take satisfaction from my work, *amigo*.' Shyness gripped her throat at the thought of saying his name, Rique; she was no longer a teenage friend of his sister's, and she sensed strongly his resentment that she came back into his father's household as someone who would see him at his most helpless.

'How dedicated you sound!' He spoke with a curl to his lip. 'Are you going to suffer with me?'

'No, I'm going to comfort you.'

'With apples?'

'If you should fancy them.'

'And with lies?'

'No.'

'You lie already, nurse.'

'Lying to my patients has never been one of my sins, *amigo*.'

'Have you any sin in you, Angel?' He gave a short laugh. 'Tell me, Maya, has your best friend grown into one of those prim and proper missionary types? Do you suppose she'll spoonfeed me and spank my backside if I don't eat my greens and spill my gravy?'

'Angie isn't at all like that,' his sister protested. 'Don't start being mean to her, Rique. Dr Romaldo insisted you were to have a nurse and if we couldn't have booked Angie then you might well have found yourself in the hands of a dragon.'

'Then am I expected to assume that Angela lives up to her name?' His soft laughter held a jeering note. 'It will hardly be wise of her to be angelic with the likes of me—I shall make mincemeat of you, Angel, if you don't watch your step.'

'I shall be busy watching yours, *amigo*,' she rejoined, increasingly aware that she must be firm with him if he was to make progress; it would be unwise to show her feelings and give way to the private distress his blunders and stumbles would evoke in her.

'So you intend to be my eyes, do you?' Rique leaned back in his chair so his dark head rested against the picturesque cane fan; his eyes held a desperate glitter in his lean dark face and every inch of him seemed to smoulder with resentment of her and the blow which fate had dealt him. There was tension in the hard shoulders under the black sweater, and in the long stretched-out legs, the gaze which was like that of an angry tiger in a trap.

'*Por infierno!*' he snarled. 'What a simpleton you must be if you think I'll submit tamely to this!' He smote a hand against his brow. 'That bomb should have completed its work and not left me like this! The two men who were with me didn't survive the blast; they were saved an awakening in hospital to find the lights had all gone out and were never going to come on again—do you imagine I don't know?'

'Oh, Rique!' his sister caught at his hand, but with an impatient movement he pulled free of her.

'Don't treat me like an infant to be pacified! Those doctors took scrap metal out of my head and I could become a drooling idiot—you know it, I know it, so let's stop pretending it is only a matter of time before I'm a man again and not a zombie stumbling around in a darkness you can't even imagine, *hermana mia*. How do I describe what blind darkness is like? It's blacker than black. It's night without the promise of morning. It's an underground tunnel with no light at the end of it! It's the grave, but I have to go on breathing——'

Angie had heard sufficient; another word along those lines and she'd be howling at his knees.

'Stop frightening your sister with such talk!' she reproved him. 'Be thankful you're alive and able to feel the sun on your skin, to hear the birds in the trees and to feel the love of a good family. Those other poor soldiers would like to be in your shoes.'

'Being led about by the hand?' His blind eyes seemed to fasten upon her face and she saw bitterness in them, and a certain look of shock as if until this moment no one else had dared to say the things she had said. 'Angel, a plate of food is placed in front of me and I might as well be eating porridge as *paella*. You have to see a slice of cured ham to be able to enjoy it; you have to see a baked potato or a cinnamon cheesecake. When a man is sightless there's no savour to a damn thing—even, I suspect, to a woman! When a man holds a woman he wants to see the look in her eyes——'

'Oh, Rique, don't torment yourself so!' Suddenly with a sob Maya ran from the garden room, and Angie found herself alone with this embittered man who had the look and shape of Rique de Zaldo but whose sightless eyes burned with a passionate agony that made them as fearful as they were striking . . . it was bewildering in a way that there was no light, no power to see in those eyes which Rique had inherited from his beautiful mother who had sadly passed away from a heart complaint before Angie had known the pleasure of meeting her.

'Maya is still much of a child,' Rique muttered. 'Our father has sheltered her in the Latin way, but you—you, Angel, have worked among the sick and the frightened and must realise a little of what I am feeling. *Por Dios*, I can't quite put together the schoolgirl image I retain of you with the adult image of a nurse in cape and cap. Would you permit me to Braille you, *niña mia*?'

Angie's instant reaction was to refuse him. To have his lean soldier's hands travelling over her might be more than she could endure without reacting to what she felt for him as a grown-up woman.

Rique sensed her hesitation and misconstrued it. 'Does it give you the creeps, Angel, the thought of being touched by a blind man's hands?'

'Not at all——' Her protest had a faintness to it, which he obviously took for the sound of rejection. He gave his sardonic laugh, so without humour as to be almost harsh.

'As I recall from the old days you had a habit of backing away from me as if I frightened the wits out of you. Your eyes would fill your face and you would look at me as if afraid I was going to bite you. Whatever induced you to come here on this mission of mercy if you retain such an aversion to me?'

A cry of protest almost made its escape from Angie's lips; she barely stopped herself from flinging her arms around him; she yearned to smooth the harsh lines from his face: yearned even more to refute his belief that he was to her an object of antipathy. She took a step as if to obey her impulse, but realised at once that it would seem to him a gesture of pity. Rique would hate her if he thought she pitied him ... he'd be scornful if he suspected that she loved him.

'I can assure you, *amigo*, that I've dealt with worse cases than yours.' Angie spoke in the cool, crisp tones of the nurse dealing with self-pity. 'Burns, for example, when people including children are brought into hospital from a fire or a scalding. I'm certainly not repelled by blindness, and if you want to Braille my features then you may do so.'

'How very generous of you, nurse,' he mocked, 'but I think I can remember that bashful face of yours and those sky-blue eyes.'

'I haven't sky-blue eyes,' she rejoined. 'You must have some other girl in mind.'

'You sound as if you disapproved.' A slightly jeering smile curled his lip. 'I have Latin blood in my veins and it runs faster and warmer than the cool British sort—ah, now I have a picture of you! Your eyes are the colour of the sea around three o'clock in the afternoon when there isn't a ripple of wind to disturb the water. They're cool and clear as ice, aren't they? Seb painted you once, but I recall that he couldn't capture the expression in your eyes.'

Time clicked its shutter and the memory was as clear as if Angie held that painting of his brother's in her hands. Seb had wanted to become an artist, but instead had made a name for himself as a director of films, working mainly in Italy and sometimes in California.

'Did Seb ever get in touch with you?' Rique had never sounded more sardonic. 'You got along with him far better than you did with me.'

'He was closer to me in age.' Angie spoke defensively, and decided not to tell Rique that his brother had contacted her when he had been in London for a film conference. They had lunched at

Motcomb's and been to see a show together. It was very true that she had always found Sebastian de Zaldo far easier to get along with; he had never made her pulse race and induced in her a breathless shyness so that she sat silent like a fool or trembled inside if Rique should look at her and pull one of her plaits.

'Don't tell me you are blushing,' Rique drawled.

'Why on earth should I blush?' Even as she spoke she felt the flow of heat in her cheeks.

'The British are very averse to personal questions, are they not?'

'Isn't everyone?' she fenced. 'I always understood that the Spanish have a certain reserve.'

'True, Angel, we have our *duende*, those strange realms of the soul where we may never share our deepest selves with anyone. Do you dream of sharing yourself with someone—my brother Seb, for instance? Did you return to the island hoping to see him again?'

'You know perfectly well why I'm here, Rique.' Her heart jolted; she had said his name and crossed a subtle barrier that brought them face to face as adults. 'I always thought Seb nicer than you, of course.'

'Of course,' he echoed mockingly. 'Seb is much nicer to women than I am; you guessed it as a child and now you're a woman you know it, don't you?'

She gazed at Rique, whose features had a fine savagery that in Seb was charming good looks. Rique looked much older than his brother though only three years separated them; he had an air of having tasted danger, the smouldering quality of a restless and unpredictable nature. It had always been there and now a real fire was burning under it.

Angie could feel the throbbing of her heart . . .

being Rique's nurse wasn't going to be easy. He wasn't nice and easy-going like Seb ... he was hurt and angry and alone in his darkness.

'The carefree days are over for all of us,' he said broodingly. 'When we romp in the sun how little we realise what may lie in store for us. Who would have thought that I would come to this, and that little Angela Hart would come here to be my guide and comfort? Fate plays strange tricks on us, eh?'

Strange, torturing tricks, she thought. She pressed a hand to the pain of suppressed tears in her throat ... memories of Rique had not been easy to erase, but time and distance had made almost bearable the ache of never seeing him except in her holiday scrapbook, caught by Seb's camera as he loped out of the sea, or lobbed a ball across the tennis net.

'Do yourself a favour!' He snarled the words. 'Go back where you came from—I want you here about as much as you want to stay! I sense it even though I can't see your face and the look in your eyes!'

'How can you be so sure about what I want?' Angie felt sharply hurt by his remark.

'Aren't most women basically the same?' He gave his sardonic laugh. 'Don't they want romance and an abiding love, someone who will be master and lover? Are you any different, or do nurses witness so much of the misery that besets mankind that they become cynical? Does too much realism gradually blot out romance for them?'

Angie had wondered about that during the journey to Bayaltar, but now she was actually here in the Residencia and face to face with Rique she knew that he was still in her heart, and because like her body her heart had grown up, her feelings had more depth and were more capable of being torn by him.

'Feelings and wounds have amazing powers of recovery,' she said. 'I'll try not to mind too much when you snap my head off, or say something sarcastic. Maya tells me that you don't eat your meals with the family.'

'I don't care to provide a poppy show when I slop food down my shirt front.' His eyes stared blindly past her shoulder. 'Being like this turns a man into a clumsy infant, and after the second attempt at sitting at the dining-table, when I upset soup all down myself, I said to hell with that and chose to eat alone.'

'Your co-ordination will improve,' she said gently. 'And I'm utterly sure that your family understand why you are clumsy. They're suffering along with you, you know.'

'Do you think I don't realise that?' He swore softly. 'I didn't wish to come home, but Padre insisted upon it. I'd have preferred staying in a military hospital until I became more capable, but he just wouldn't listen to reason. He flew to Spain and brought me home himself. *Dios*, he's a tough *hombre*!'

'You take after him,' Angie murmured. 'Because he's in you, you won't allow blindness to become a handicap——'

'What else is it?' he broke in harshly. 'It's as if walls have closed around me and I can't find the way out— and I'm not just blind, am I? I have had their knives inside my head, so, Angel, what are you going to do if I suddenly become violent and start smashing things? Are you going to be the one to put me in a straitjacket when I turn into a crazy man?'

'Nothing of the sort is going to happen!' she exclaimed. 'Stop saying such things!'

'Don't you care to hear the truth?' he jeered. 'Supposing one day when you and I are alone you find my hands around your throat? They say that when people go out of their mind they turn on the person who helps them.'

'You're talking wild nonsense just to try and frighten me,' she reproved him, but was glad that he couldn't see the distress in her eyes as they rested upon the raw scarring of his temple where the bomb fragments had penetrated. If any of those fragments had bedded themselves where the knife hadn't dared to disturb them, then Rique certainly lived in the shadow of violence of death and he was far too intelligent not to realise it. The awareness was there in his eyes, a shadow haunting his blindness.

'I frighten myself, Angel.' Ash spilled from his *cigarillo* and left a grey smudge on his black sweater. She saw that he might burn himself, and quietly she took the stub away and dropped it into an ashtray on the cane table beside his chair.

'*Gracias, mi muchache.*' Suddenly and swiftly his hand gripped her wrist and the next moment he was pulling her against his legs. Angie stumbled and instantly his arm was around her waist and he was forcing her on to his knees, a look of mocking savagery joining forces in his face.

'Please don't——'

'Frightened of a blind man?' His hand travelled up her body to her neck, where his fingers found her nape and fastened upon it. 'I can feel you trembling, Angel—why the devil did you come to Bayaltar?

Curiosity? Misplaced loyalty? Boredom with your work in London?'

'Y-you have a cruel tongue, Rique!' She struggled to get away, but his strength was far superior to hers, added to which she was enfeebled by his nearness and his touch. She could feel her own weakness and her longing to curl her arms about his neck and press her lips to his scars and his blind eyes. It was a weakness she had to fight even as his grip was forcing her close to him until the hard line of his lips was only a breath away from the tremor of her lips.

'Perhaps a kiss from you might sweeten me, eh?' Abruptly and brutally he found her mouth with his and twisted his lips against hers, stifling the cry of protest that arose in her throat as she felt the grinding insolence of his kiss. It seemed to go on and on until Angie felt her breath fading, then with a harsh sort of laugh Rique pushed her away from him . . . she stumbled backwards and gazed at him with great distress in her eyes, a hand against her tingling lips.

'Now you know what to expect from me if you persist in staying here.' The lamplight on his face seemed to intensify its look of shadowed menace. A black strand of hair lay across his brow and his sightless eyes burned into her even though they couldn't see her. Anger was etched into his features, also torment and actual hatred of those who could see lay in his eyes, points of flame from twin pits of hell . . . the hell which Angie had chosen to share.

'You aren't the first recalcitrant patient I've had to deal with,' she told him bravely.

'Recalcitrant?' He laughed sarcastically. 'What big words you use!'

'Stubborn, unmanageable and rebellious,' she added.

'And you imagine you're going to tame me, nurse?'

'Tigers can't be tamed, but they can be dealt with.'

'With a whip?' The thought seemed to amuse him. 'The picture of my nurse standing over me with a whip is highly provocative. I think I'd prefer that to the soothing hand on the brow and the lying reassurances that one day I'm going to wake up with the sunlight in my eyes. Prove to me that you have the *sal* to take me on, Angel. Tell me what no one else has dared to put into words . . . tell me I'm down in Hades for the remainder of my days.'

Angie wanted with all her heart to tell him that he wasn't always going to be in the dark; she wanted like everyone else to say it was only a matter of time before he regained his sight and could throw away his cane. Instead she had to compromise.

'I haven't yet spoken with Dr Romaldo so I don't really know all the details of your case. I do know that mystifying things can happen if people have faith and hope and don't let themselves dwell in hell. There are worse afflictions than blindness——'

'Quite.' He clipped the word as if his lips were shears. 'There's madness, isn't there? The raving lunacy that can turn a man into an animal you called me a tiger, didn't you?'

'Yes, but I meant——'

' "The tiger's howl shall oft be heard
    Sounding through tower and dome," '
he quoted.

' "Something superb, impetuous, resistless," '
Angie silently completed, words from the pen of Char-

lotte Brontë and strangely apt where Rique was concerned. He would resist every effort she made to help him come to terms with his blindness, yet she knew he had the courage to put up a fight if only he found the will to do so. But like a shifting shadow in a corner there lurked a spectre more deadly than his night-dark days and his moonless nights.

Rique de Zaldo lived in fear that a fragment of metal might have damaged his brain and would one day send him out of his mind. Angie knew he would rather be dead if such an appalling thing should happen . . . and if it happened she knew she loved him enough to grant his death wish.

'So,' he leaned back in his chair and stretched his legs, 'you return to Bayaltar and intend to take me on?'

'I certainly won't encourage you to brood like Hamlet among your ghosts,' she assured him.

'I shall damn well brood if I want to,' he growled. 'As I said a while ago, I'd prefer you to go on back to your bedpans and bottles. All I want is to be left in peace.'

'So you can vegetate? I never took you for a shirker, Rique. I thought your motto was that the man who dares is the man who wins.'

'He who dares,' he drew a finger across his eyelids, 'loses.'

'You haven't lost everything,' she argued. 'You have all your other senses and it's up to you to make them work for you.'

'You know it isn't just the blindness——' His breath caught in his throat as if his secret fear rose up chokingly.

'I know, Rique. I realise how you must feel——'

'Do you really?' His lips twisted. 'You are young and healthy and you don't lie awake at night counting the hours. You don't lie in the dark waiting for your mind to give way.'

'*Amigo*,' she reached out and caught him by the hand, clasping it and then pressing her palm to his in the holy palmer's kiss of sympathy. 'You aren't alone, Rique. You've only to call me day or night and I'll come to you. My hand is yours to hold.'

'Only your hand?' He spoke mockingly. 'Spare me your pity!'

'I don't pity you——'

'Be sure you mean it, Angel.'

'You were always very proud, Rique.'

'It's my Spanish blood. Look, there's a bottle and a glass on the table near my chair, will you pour me a drink?'

Angie lifted the bottle and looked at the label. It was Spanish cognac and probably as strong as fire water. He listened as she poured. 'I said a drink, not a spoonful of the stuff. It isn't medicine.'

'Drink never solved anyone's problems.' She handed him the glass and watched the way his fingers locked about it.

'It may not solve them, but it helps me to live with them. *Salud*.'

'I have to go and unpack my case,' she said. 'I'll see you later, Rique.'

'Doubtless.' He lifted the cognac to his lips. 'I'm not going anywhere, except, perhaps, to the devil.'

'Rique——'

'Don't lecture me, Angel. Go and unpack your frillies.'

She sighed and left him sitting there in the lamplit garden room.

CHAPTER TWO

ANGIE left Rique alone with his thoughts and his cognac and walked out into the hall; her eyes were shadowed as she stood unseeing in front of a large painting of poppies in a brass jug. She could feel herself trembling inside from her meeting with Rique, their conversation and the kiss she had resisted.

Why had she resisted when she felt the way she did about him? Sadly she knew the answer; he hadn't kissed her because he cared for her, or desired her, he had meant to try and alarm her so she would leave the Residencia and return to London rather than face the task of looking after him.

But Rique didn't yet know that she could be as stubborn as he . . . he certainly had no idea that she was in love with him. The love was lodged in her heart and quite painfully alive and kicking as she stood there in the hall, hearing the deep tick-tock of the grandfather clock and distant sounds from the kitchen where dinner was being prepared.

'Shall I show you where you will be sleeping?'

Angie gave a visible start and swung round to face the owner of the voice. She recognised instantly the young woman who stood facing her clad in an exquisite lace blouse with a long deep-green velvet skirt. A lovelock was coiled against her cheekbone, dark in contrast to skin pale as a lotus petal. There was pastel shadow on her rather heavy eyelids, and flecks of green in her eyes as they wandered over Angie.

Ysabel Ferrandos was distantly related to the Zaldo family and had been adopted into it long ago, almost a sister to Maya and her brothers . . . except that Angie had always suspected that Ysabel would like a much closer relationship to Rique de Zaldo.

But that had been in the old days, of course. Before Rique had been injured and blinded . . . instinct told Angie that Ysabel was basically cool and calculating and hardly the type to desire a blind husband who would need her protection in a number of ways, as well as compassion and tolerance.

'Have you forgotten me?' Ysabel's lips curled into a smile that wasn't exactly friendly. 'You I remember very well . . . your hair stayed fair, unless you help it along with the aid of a blonde tint?'

'Fortunately I don't have to bother with anything like that.' Angie's own smile was quizzical as she ran her gaze over Ysabel's hair, artfully arranged with an auburn tint to it, highlighting its Latin darkness.

'So you became a nurse.' Ysabel stroked a hand down her jawbone; green stones glinted in her earlobes and she looked soignée and ready for the evening meal which Angie knew was always eaten in style in the large dining-room at a big oval table covered in Spanish lace, silver and glassware.

'I'm surprised you had the nerve to take up nursing,' Ysabel went on. 'You always seemed a rather timid creature, something which always amused Rique. Now, of all things, you are here to take care of him. Have you yet seen him?'

Angie nodded. She didn't wish to discuss Rique with Ysabel and so she turned towards the staircase. 'I have to go up and unpack and tidy myself for dinner. Has Maya arranged for me to have my old room?'

'No.' Ysabel's voice had a sudden edge to it. 'She persuaded Don Carlos that you should be within call of Rique in case he should need you in the night, so you are to sleep in the room next to his suite. I hope the proximity won't disturb you . . . that is if he still makes you feel timid?'

'It would be absurd for a nurse to be timid.' Angie made her way up the mahogany staircase with the shining handrail that curved up gracefully to the orna-mental iron that was set along the *galeria* overlooking the long drop to the hall. She could feel Ysabel at her heels and hear the long velvet skirt trailing the treads.

'I know the way,' she said, 'if Rique still sleeps in that big corner room overlooking the sea.'

'When would you have been in Rique's bedroom?' Ysabel's mockery had an edge to it.

'All of us were still at school when I used to come here for the holidays,' Angie rejoined. 'Going in and out of each other's bedrooms was innocent enough in those days.'

'No doubt you would think so,' Ysabel drawled. 'Perhaps you never noticed that Rique was no callow schoolboy . . . you say you have seen him, so what do you make of him now?'

Angie paused there on the *galeria* and her gaze was reflective. She hadn't regarded Rique as callow and she could remember as if it were yesterday the agile way he used to leap these very stairs, possessed of the raking stride of a man going places.

'Rique has been through hell and I'll do my utmost

to help him recover,' she said, keeping her emotions firmly in check. 'I know he's become a difficult and bitter man, but I'm trained to cope with his sort. I'm not nervous or intimidated by him.'

'I find it intriguing that you should hurry to Bay-altar in order to be Rique's nurse.' Ysabel's green-flecked eyes were narrow and searching as a cat's when it scents a mouse. 'Was it sentimentality that brought you back here, or something a little more personal?'

'I came because Maya and her father asked me to come. Don Carlos was always kind to me and I want to repay him for his hospitality.' Angie walked on, rounding a bend of the *galeria* in the businesslike way of a nurse. But Ysabel wasn't to be shaken off and she actually followed Angie into the bedroom she had been given to sleep in, where only a wall would separate her from Rique so she would hear him if he stumbled and fell, or was restless in the night and needed a painkiller. She had seen the lines etched into his face and they told her that he still suffered a certain amount of pain.

Angie flicked on the wall-lights of her room and breathed the scent of lavender bags and fresh bed linen. It was a charming, antique room, with burnished furniture, thick colourful rugs on the floor and an intricate lace throwover across the bed, which had tall twisted posts and netting tucked back behind the big plump pillows. Her suitcase had been brought upstairs and stood ready for unpacking on a stool at the foot of the fourposter.

A soft sigh of pleasure stole from Angie's lips. She was again in the same house as Rique, and despite the difficulties in store for her, she wouldn't have changed this moment had a charming tycoon wanted to whisk her off to a tropical paradise to a life of total ease and luxury.

Ysabel leaned against one of the bedposts and watched as Angie unlocked her suitcase. She had packed in haste and brought sufficient clothing for her immediate needs. There were plenty of shops on the island and she could always go shopping for any additions to her wardrobe. She took scant notice of the look on Ysabel's face as she put away her frillies, as Rique had called them, and hung her few dresses in the closet.

'I imagine you will be wearing your uniform most of the time?' Ysabel remarked, touching with a silvered fingertip the starched cap which Angie placed on the bed beside a navy-blue dress.

'Most of the time I shall be on duty,' Angie replied.

'How conscientious you sound!' Ysabel slid her eyes over Angie's face. 'I thought nurses were always being dated by doctors and the male patients who take a fancy to them.'

'That sort of thing happens more often in television serials than real life.' Angie placed her few lotions and scents on the dressing-table. 'In real nursing there isn't much glamour and very little time for romances with those tall, dark, magnetic doctors who exist only in the magazines.'

'Rique isn't a doctor, but he certainly is tall, dark and magnetic,' Ysabel murmured, her eyes intent upon Angie. 'You have noticed that, eh?'

'Of course.' Angie made herself sound casual. 'He takes very much after his father, doesn't he? Apart from his eyes—their colour, I mean, not their present condition.'

'Is it likely to be a permanent condition?' Ysabel studied one of her slender hands, which looked as if its main occupation was the creaming of her skin and the grooming of her sleek auburn-touched hair.

'I haven't yet discussed Rique's case with Dr Romaldo.' Angie arranged her brush and comb set on the lace mat in front of the dressing-table mirror, noticing from a brief look into the mirror that her face was tense and a 'trifle drawn, an outward indication of her inner concern for Rique. She wished Ysabel would go, but the Spanish girl was obviously curious and intent on delving into Angie's reasons for coming back to Bayaltar.

'You medical people are always so secretive, are you not?' Ysabel's eyes glittered cat-green, and then she gave a shrug. 'Don Carlos is greatly concerned, that's why you are here. Don't imagine Rique asked for you!'

'That's the last thing I'd imagine.' Angie thrust from her forehead the wave of hair that had a tendency to flop forward; she believed it made her look untidy, but in reality it was rather fetching, that sheen of gold above the gravity of her grey-blue eyes.

'Is Rique not pleased that Don Carlos has asked you here?'

'Rique is angry with the world at the present time,' Angie replied.

'So already he gives you a little bit of hell, eh?' Ysabel's lips curled into a smile, as if she delighted in the image of Rique de Zaldo being biting and sarcastic to Angie. Angie wasn't surprised by such a reaction; she was well aware that Ysabel had a jealous disposition which she had often revealed in the past.

'I shouldn't wish to be a nurse.' Ysabel moved her gaze around Angie's bedroom, her eyes coming to rest on the door that adjoined the apartment which was Rique's. 'Don Carlos wouldn't like me to go out to work, no more than he allows Maya to do so. He has plenty of money and his position as Governor to consider, apart from which it pleases him to have us about the house. The thing that is so satisfactory about Latin men is their protectiveness of their women. Being Latin myself I don't object to this attitude as much as Englishwomen seem to. Men in my opinion are the stronger, better equipped sex, so why shouldn't they rule the roost? I think it's stupid of women not to like being protected—are you one of those, Angela? Are you the type who likes to think she doesn't need a man to take care of her?'

'I like to think I'm not quite a nitwit.' Angie closed her suitcase and put it away in the bottom of the closet. 'I happen to believe that a man and a woman are meant to be friends on all levels, not master and slave.'

'Then you wouldn't like to be dominated by someone—let us say, Don Carlos?' Ysabel strolled to the dressing-table and studied her reflection in the mirror, which was shaped like a shield. She stroked a finger across an eyebrow and smiled through the glass at Angie; a faintly supercilious smile.

'Don Carlos is a great gentleman,' Angie replied, 'but even he couldn't convince me that it's better for a woman to be kept under glass like an exotic plant, only being allowed the sunshine of his approval and petting.'

'Really?' Ysabel drawled. 'You sound so emphatic that I am almost convinced you mean what you say.

My conviction is that no matter the woman, whether she be Latin or otherwise, there is deep inside her the longing to have this—shall we say?—rather arrogant possessiveness shown by a man. I believe all women—if they are real women—have this secret longing to be jealously possessed, and Latin men are good at it!'

'I'm sure they are,' Angie said drily.

'You are still a virgin, are you not, Angela?'

The question this time was unexpected, and somehow so blatant that Angie blushed, the hot scarlet warmth rising out of the neck of her white shirt and up over the skin of her face to the roots of her fair hair. She felt mortified by the blush, and the mockery that flickered in Ysabel's eyes—the so-called sheltered Latin girl who should be the one to be blushing and virginal. Angie on the other hand was a nurse to whom the biological mysteries of the human body were well known; but it was a fact she couldn't deny that she had kept her own integrity intact. Had she done so because of Rique? Because always he had been there in her mind and in her heart? There had certainly been occasions when men had tried to overcome her inclination to keep herself from being cheapened by the casual encounters other girls indulged in as if they were going to the Tandoori for a take-away dinner. Angie enjoyed Tandoori dinners, but she had certainly turned her back on casual affairs.

Ysabel laughed, for her sharp eyes hadn't missed the coming and going of Angie's give-away blush. She brushed a hand almost sensuously down the deep-green velvet of her skirt. 'You were always a rather quaint child and I see you haven't changed, except to look older on the outside. I really have the feeling that you came back to Bayaltar just to be near Rique, even though he couldn't care less about you being here.'

The Spanish girl came towards Angie, who had to force herself not to back away from something almost menacing in Ysabel's manner. 'Rique might be blind, but he has a quick mind, so you had better be careful, Angela, that he doesn't guess how you feel about him.'

Angie's heart missed a beat, but she strove not to pull her eyes away from Ysabel's probing gaze. 'I feel concerned for him, much as Maya and his father feel concerned,' she said, and by some effort of will she managed to keep her voice steady. 'He's the son of Don Carlos, who opened his house to me when I was young and didn't have relatives of my own to visit during the school holidays. I remember his kindness with gratitude, and that's why I'm here, Ysabel, and I'd appreciate it if you kept your ridiculous opinions to yourself. If you said such things to Rique, he might think you were being cruel to him.'

'Cruel?' Ysabel echoed. 'Why should he think any such thing?'

'Surely you can see why? Rique believes he's become a figure of pity and I'm going to have a hard enough task gaining his trust and confidence without anyone alienating him against me. He needs help— competent, trained help such as I can give him, so I must ask you to keep your hints and innuendoes to yourself, Ysabel. They have no basis——'

'If it pleases you to say so, Angela.' Ysabel strolled to the door leading out on to the *galeria*, her suggestive words trailing back over her shoulder with chiffon-soft mockery. 'I believe you are besotted with

him; why else would you come flying from London to
be near him in his hour of need? I will tell you what
Rique needs, my dear.' Ysabel stood there in the doorway, a mixture of insolence and dislike in her eyes. 'It
isn't a do-gooder in a starched uniform to hold his
hand and tranquillise him. You'll be sleeping right
next door to him, so don't be surprised if one night he
should let you know his real wants and needs. You're a
nurse and yet you look at me with such cool and innocent eyes. He wants someone to hold him in the
dark so he can stop thinking—there is something very
potent about sex, Angela, it can shut the door of the
mind and blot out the realities for as long as it lasts.
You wouldn't know, would you?'

'Would you?' Angie retaliated.

'It would be amazing if I did not know.' Ysabel gave
a soft and knowing laugh. 'You came to spend holidays with Rique's family; I have lived here most of my
life and grown up at his side. I leave you to imagine
the rest. Rique, as you are aware, has always been attractive to the opposite sex. They have always turned
in the street to look at him, and they have always been
inclined to let him have his own way with them. There
have been exceptions—those he hasn't felt attracted to.
You are probably in that category, my dear Angela.
Latin men like the warm look, not the cool one, and
you generate a touch-me-not quality. Did you know?'

Angie couldn't be bothered to answer and with one
of those sinuous shrugs of hers Ysabel strolled away,
leaving her words to sink into Angie's mind. She saw
the logic in Ysabel's reasoning, about his dark and
empty nights, and she knew very well that he had
never made an advance to her except in the flower

room tonight, and the motive for that had been to try and frighten her away.

Angie was resolved; nothing was going to make her run away, neither Rique's antagonism nor Ysabel's insinuation that she and Rique had been more than proxy brother and sister.

The very thought stabbed her like a knife, but if it was true then she had to live with it; if she had suspected something of the sort when she was a mere sixteen, then there was every possibility that Rique had been involved with Ysabel, and even yet there might be something between them. It certainly didn't please Ysabel that Angie would be living and sleeping in such close proximity to him.

Angie sighed. Poor Rique, the nights must seem like eternity to him, especially when he couldn't fall off to sleep. Each day he lived through twenty-four hours of darkness, alone within himself, looking inwardly because he could no longer enjoy the distraction of looking at people and objects, sky and land, trees and birds. There would be times when he felt a deep need to share his active senses with someone; the sense of touch in particular, kindling into the desire to hold, to kiss, to love until the racking fears were swept away like the tide from the shore.

Still troubled by her thoughts, Angie made her way to the bathroom, the *salón de aguas* as it was called in this Spanish house—hall of waters, a grand description of a bathroom which always used to amuse her. There was something grand about the Spanish language, just as there was something of grandeur about its men, as if the dash and daring of their *conquistador* forebears still ran strong and active in their veins. It was that strain in Rique which had led him into the army, for he had taken a commission after serving his term of national service and had been discharged as a lieutenant.

She wished she could have seen him in his uniform, tall, supple, striding along with that dark head held proudly high. Now he must go through life haltingly, and the thought filled Angie with pain.

With an angry twist of her wrist she turned the hot-water tap and steam filled the *salón de aguas*. How cruel fate could be, lurking like a wolf to spring at the throat of a man's hopes and dreams! Water gushed into the king-sized tub which someone as long-legged as Rique needed. Thick bathmats clung to the mosaic tiles of the floor and immense soft-textured Indian towels hung over the heated rail. The large wall mirror misted as Angie shed her clothes and stepped white and slender into the welcoming water, to which she had added a handful of the sea-green bath salts that promised on the label of the jar all sorts of soothing sensations.

She sank back into the water, resting her head upon the rubber cushion placed so conveniently for a bath-time snooze. Stretched out like this she only reached three-quarters of the way down the tub. Rique's long frame would stretch all the way, and she couldn't stop her mind from tracing his image, nor her body from recalling his hard-muscled thighs when he had pulled her down into his arms and forced upon her that grinding kiss which had bruised her lips against her teeth.

Close to him like that she had felt the power and the pull of his strong body, the barely checked savagery that stemmed from his need to hurt anyone who could see the sunlight and the pageantry of life in clear colours and shapes.

The tears she had suppressed welled into her eyes and overflowed down her cheeks, and the pain of what he was going through distorted her face as she wept unashamedly in the privacy of the bathroom. She let herself cry, knowing that if she released the tears she would reach some level of calmness and be able to cope with the job that lay ahead of her. For several tortured minutes the hot tears kept coming and she bathed them away with her sponge. It wouldn't do to appear at the dining-table with puffy eyelids; the sharp-sighted Ysabel would guess that she had been crying for Rique and would be jeeringly amused.

'Crying for a man who doesn't want you here,' her green eyes would jeer.

'Stop now, you idiot!' Angie chastened herself, and splashed water into her face until her eyes were tingling. She wanted, with a shy urgency, to keep her feelings for Rique to herself, and though she was disposed to be fair in her judgments of people, she couldn't pretend to like Ysabel. She had been something of a troublemaker when they were all young, and Maya hadn't yet confided to Angie how she had come to break off her friendship with the musician who had been playing guitar and singing at the Castelo de Madrigal, a big tourist hotel on the island.

Ysabel had always been inclined to make mischief between Don Carlos and his children, and Angie hadn't forgotten how bossy she had been towards Maya when they were younger, nor her habit of borrowing Maya's belongings and never returning them. It was a trait which might include men now the proxy sisters were grown up, especially if happiness in love was eluding Ysabel. She was sensuously attractive, but she lacked Maya's sweet and sensitive nature.

Angie stepped from the bath and wrapped one of the enormous towels around her. She wiped the steamed-up mirror and peered into it for any telltale sign of tears; her eyes still looked a trifle weepy, but a touch of eye make-up would, she hoped, repair the ravages.

She tied the sash of her robe, opened the door and stepped out on to the *galeria* . . . the next instant a gasp of alarm escaped her as she came into collision with a tall figure, a cane poised seekingly in front of him.

'Rique!' She pressed back against the wall. 'I—I didn't see you!'

'It's for me to say that!' He touched her with his cane. 'I smell my bath salts, so I imagine you've been wallowing in them.'

'I didn't know they were yours.' Her skin was prickling at his dark proximity. 'I saw the jar on a shelf and helped myself.'

'Already you make yourself at home, eh?' His lips took their mordant twist and his brows were drawn blackly together above his eyes that gazed at her as if he could see her. The look was so disconcerting that Angie drew together the borders of her robe, a foolish yet involuntary action.

The next moment Rique proved how acute his hearing had become. 'I heard the slither of silk against skin,' the tone of voice was sardonic. 'You've just had a bath and you are wearing only a robe. In case you're blushing, Angel, I can't see you, but I have a mental image of you—your damp hair flops above your eyes and you have just tied yet another knot in the sash of your bathrobe. What a prude you've grown into if you need to hide yourself from a blind man!'

'It's just—' her blush deepened, 'just that I haven't yet become used to the fact that you're——'

'That I'm blind as a bat!' he broke in. 'That I have to rely on my nose, my ears and my memory where women are concerned. What colour is the silk?'

'A sort of dusky rose,' she said, knowing he referred to her robe.

'Has it batwing sleeves that reveal your arms when you lift them to brush your hair?'

'It has wide sleeves——' Her eyes were magnetised by his face, the flare to his nostrils and the throb of a vein in his temple. Part of her wanted to retreat when he moved towards her; she could see his hand groping for her and she made no move when he found her shoulder and closed his fingers upon her.

'I'm going to Braille you whether you want it or not,' he said.

She stood there dumbly, feeling the devil urge in him to run his touch over her while she was un-protected by her uniform. Something in her wanted it to happen, clad as she was in nothing but a silk robe, her hair in soft, tumbling disarray. Each separate nerve in her seemed aware of him, dangerous and threatening despite his blind eyes.

'You will agree that it's hardly fair,' he murmured, 'that you can see me while I am in the dark about you. The last time I saw you, you were a child in cotton shorts and sandals.'

'Then you had better get it over with.' Angie had

never felt so defenceless in her life and was quite
unable to resist as he Brailled her features with his
lean fingers and trailed them down the side of her neck
to the V of her robe. His touch lingered there a
moment and she watched him in a kind of daze,
trembling slightly as his fingers travelled over the
silk that clung in soft folds to her body.

Suddenly he pressed her to the wall, his cane striking her ankle as it fell from his grasp. Her breath came
quickly as he bared one of her shoulders and found it
with his lips. Oh God, she had lain awake at night and
wondered what it would feel like to be in Rique de
Zaldo's arms . . . now she was in his arms, but he
wasn't whispering the crazy, loving endearments she
had dreamed about.

What was happening in this dim corner of the house
was Rique reaching out in his darkness for the mind-
less relief of sensual contact . . . Ysabel had said it
might happen and, feeling suddenly cheap, Angie
thrust his hand away.

'That's enough!' she gasped. 'You go too far when
you Braille a person!'

'Who knows how far—if it wasn't that I'm blind.'

'What do you mean by that?' Her hands shook as
she drew her robe tightly around her; her knees felt
equally weak.

'I can understand your rejection—it's the second
time, isn't it?' He loomed above her, black sweater to
his chin, black brows shading his brooding face and
mouth touched by a twist of bitterness. 'What girl
wants to be kissed by a man with stones in his head
instead of a pair of eyes?'

'Rique!' The awfulness of his words struck her like
stones. 'How can you say such a thing?'

'All too easily.' He swung round so he was facing the stairs instead of his suite. '*Dios*, I seem to have lost my sense of direction—can you bear to lead me to my room, nurse?'

'Of course I can.' Angie picked up his cane, then placed his hand upon her arm so she could guide him without propelling him. She opened the door of his suite and automatically switched on the lights. The twist to Rique's mouth became more pronounced as he heard the click of the switch.

'I don't need the light, unless you're thinking of joining me,' he said.

'It was just a reflex action on my part,' she replied. 'Will you be all right? I have to dress for dinner— Rique, why not come downstairs and have dinner with your family?'

'I prefer to eat alone.' He walked forward into his bedroom, where the furniture was positioned against the walls so he wouldn't stumble over it. His fourposter bed was between the windows where the curtains billowed in the evening air through the openings. Angie smelled the sea and guessed that in the silence of the night the sound of the sea would drift to him. Rique would lie in the darkness and listen to the swish of the waves, so free a sound while he lay trapped by his blindness. She knew how bitter must be his frustration ... how awful that bottomless pit that let in no chink of light ... and light was the colour of hope.

'Don't allow yourself to become withdrawn from those who love you,' she pleaded. 'You must know how much your family cares for you.'

'I'm sure they pity me.' He spoke harshly. 'Most people, no matter how well intentioned, become im-

patient of the halt and the blind; the deaf and dumb.
Life has an urgency about it which sweeps aside anything which stands uncertain in its path. Angel, you
demonstrated yourself that the afflicted are a bore, but
I don't blame you for your reaction. You are here because my father wanted you here, understood? I hope
you won't regret coming back out of a sentimental
sense of obligation because you spent your school holidays with us. School is out. Playtime is over for me.'

'Don't talk like a defeatist, Rique,' she begged. 'I
know you've been through hell and I know it isn't possible for the sighted to comprehend what it feels like
not to be able to see objects and faces, but you have
your physical strength——'

'For how long?' he demanded. 'Just how long does
it take to go out of your mind? You're a nurse, so you
tell me—if you dare!'

'Rique——' Her hand reached of its own accord and
as she clasped his arm she felt the tension of his
muscles, like cords to her touch. 'You shut yourself
away from people and brood too much. You're alive
and you have to join the stream of life again, even if at
first you take slow steps instead of quick ones. Do you
go outside the house at all? Have you been into town
since you came home?'

'Hell, no!' He flung her hand from his arm. 'I don't
intend to go shambling among the crowds with a cane,
aware that people are looking at me and thinking,
"Poor devil, I feel sorry for him, but let him not come
near me!" Oh yes, that's what people say to themselves,
Angel. They think what I've got is contagious!'

'Don't talk rubbish!' she exclaimed, the pain inside
her making her voice sharp.

'Rubbish, is it?' His expression was savage. 'When I

touched you tonight you had the shakes—you reacted as if a leper had put his hands on you. Go and get dressed. Go and have your dinner. If you had an ounce of sense you'd fly back to England and carry on with your life. Maya had no right to drag you here and throw you in my company. I know what I've become. I know what I look like. I can feel the scars.'

'They aren't as bad as you think, Rique. A little plastic surgery will do wonders——'.

'And turn the Beast into Prince Charming?' he jeered. 'Run along, child, or you'll be late for your dinner.'

'I'm not a child, Rique.'

'It's the way I remember you. My memory is still intact.'

'You Brailled me, and that must have told you that I've grown up.'

'I found out what I wanted to know, that when a blind man touches a girl she hates every second of his clumsiness. Don't treat me like an idiot before it happens—and that's an order, nurse.'

'Don't behave like a bully,' she rejoined. 'It's those I find obnoxious.'

'I don't really care a damn how you find me,' he said cuttingly. 'Don't get the idea I took hold of you because I felt a thing for you. You never were my type.'

'I know, Rique, so don't treat me like an idiot.' She said it bravely enough but was glad he couldn't see the hurt in her eyes. 'I'm aware that your sole reason was to try and make me quit this job even before I've started it. But I'm no quitter, so bite on that and chew it well before you swallow it.'

She actually silenced him for a second or two, then

he allowed himself a brief sardonic laugh. 'So you did grow up, Angela Hart.'

'Of course I grew up, Rique de Zaldo. Did you imagine I arrived here all wide-eyed and apprehensive, my bucket and spade in my hand?'

'Perhaps so,' he ruminated. 'It's the way you walk through the mists of my memory, in cotton shorts and bare feet, your plaits coming undone. What became of the plaits?'

'I had them cut off because I knew you'd want to pull them again.'

'Pity,' he drawled. 'They'd have come in useful for leading me about.'

'If you don't want to be led about, Rique, then it's up to you to learn your own way around. Plenty of blind people manage remarkably well.'

'How fortunate for them!'

'You're an intelligent man, Rique. You'll learn quickly how to adjust to a new way of life——'

'My old way of life suited me, *niña mia*.' His face was rigid with resistance. 'I was an excellent soldier and I wanted to go on being one. By the Virgin, you might have developed the shape of a woman, but you still seem to think with the romantic mind of a schoolgirl! I had what I wanted, and now I have nothing that pertains to it. I feel as if that bomb blasted me out into limbo, and you come along with your proper little maxims, mouthing them as if they hold all the answers to my problems. Start living again, you tell me—at what? Basket weaving?'

Angie sighed and knew that right now there was no reasoning with him. They had to become reacquainted. He had to learn to accept her as a friend he could trust, and it would take time and toleration.

'You know better than that,' she said quietly. 'I'm going to my room—is there someone who helps you shave and dress?'

'Yes—Primitivo. You probably remember him. He's an islander who has always worked for my father.'

'Yes, I remember.'

'Just don't forget any of the things I've said—understood?'

He turned away from her, and again she sighed and walked to the door and left him alone with his bitter thoughts; his dwelling upon a life he considered over and done with.

Angie felt anxious, and yet at the same time challenged. She couldn't allow someone like Rique to become a recluse, shut away with his despair and his fear of losing his mind as well as his sight. She couldn't be soft with him like his family, a very Latin one to whom, as the eldest son of the *hidalgo*, he had his rights and privileges. If he chose not to be intruded upon, then that choice was respected by them. Angie considered herself in a different category; much as she cared for Rique it was her duty to try and rekindle those vital forces which had been so much a part of him.

If conflict was to be the order of the day, then she'd enter into battle with him. She'd rouse him somehow, even if she made him hate her, and hurt her.

CHAPTER THREE

ANGIE was putting the finishing touches to her toilette when the dinner gong resounded through the Residencia.

How that familiar sound swept the years aside; as if it were only a day ago she recalled the rush of feet on the stairs as the *hidalgo*'s sons raced down them to be first at the table, where Don Carlos would rebuke them for their lack of dignity, but with a smile lurking deep in his dark eyes.

'One would think that you boys had not seen food for days,' he would remark. 'The pair of you have the appetites of recruits who have been force-marched!'

A tiny smile came and went in Angie's eyes as she fastened the string of pearls Carlos de Zaldo had given her that last Christmas she had stayed here. She smoothed the long skirt of her dress, simply styled but a glowing shade of burgundy that suited her skin and hair, showing off their fairness and giving her the look of poise she needed so badly.

Outside her room she glanced at the adjacent door; she hated the thought of Rique sitting alone in the dark with a dinner tray, but it was best if she left him alone tonight. Tomorrow he might be a little more amenable to her presence, but right now he felt resentful that he had need of a nurse . . . like some infant who hadn't yet found his feet.

Angie made her way down the graceful staircase to the hall . . . a tall figure was standing there as if awaiting her, clad in a well-cut dinner-suit, a proud set to his iron-grey head, a figure stroking his thick black moustache in a way Angie remembered so well.

This was Rique's distinguished father, the Governor-General of the island, with a power in his face which he had passed on to his son. It was their eyes which were so different; the father's were vitally alive while Rique's grey gaze was blind as ice.

The femininity in Angie warmed to the lithe regality of Don Carlos; the old admiration stirred for those stern features that masked a warm heart.

'My dear child,' he held out his hands to her, 'how good to see you again, and how charmingly you have grown up! My house is yours, be welcome in it!'

When the warm hands clasped hers and drew them to the moustached lips Angie did indeed feel welcomed.

'I'm happy to see you again, *señor*.' She smiled with a touch of shyness, for like Rique the Don had the kind of Latin personality that made a woman very aware of being female. 'I wish I was back here as a visitor and not as a nurse.'

'Ah yes.' His eyes became sombre. 'You have seen my son, eh? What is your impression of him?'

'That he's hiding himself away, and that's the worst thing possible for him to do. I think my first task, Don Carlos, will be to persuade him to get out of the house for a few jaunts around the island in order to get himself used to his new strange world. He's so proud and so afraid of the mixture of pity and retreat that people feel for the blind. It isn't rejection, as he believes, it's fear on their part of providing an obstacle he might fall over.'

'I see you have given thought to the matter, my child.' Don Carlos's strong hands gripped hers until she came close to wincing. 'There has to be some hope that he will see again! Rique is the son of my bones and my brain, and I doubt if I could face such an affliction.'

'If it's to be permanent, *señor*, then it must be faced,' Angie said quietly. 'You must have spoken with the surgeon who operated upon your son—did he give you any reason for hope?'

Rique's father gazed across the hall in an unseeing way, then he shook his iron-grey head. 'Medics can be so exasperating, they have a way of never committing themselves to a specific answer. I was told that Rique is lucky to be alive. I was informed that there was some penetration of the brain by bomb fragments. The surgeon seemed uncertain of the outcome of that! I was, however, permitted to bring him home providing I agreed to have a nurse for him resident in the house. Maya suggested at once that you were the best person possible and it's our good fortune that your duties permitted you to come to us. I am most grateful, Angela. It was kind of you to wish to help old friends in their need.'

'That's what friends are for, *señor*.' Her smile was quavery and emotion threatened to bring the hot tears to her eyes again. She swallowed the lump that came into her throat and it hurt. 'I shall do my utmost to help Rique adjust to being blind.'

'*Ay Dios*!' Pain was reflected on the Don's strong face. 'Why should such a thing happen to my son, eh? What did I do that offended the Almighty? My boy has fought in battles and earned his commission with a decoration for bravery, but this—this thing that he fights now, it has cast him very low, Angela. The things he enjoyed were so physical . . . do you know that he has the fencing title of *maître d'armes*? And how he could swim——'

'He'll still be able to swim, *señor*.' Angie spoke eagerly. 'The ocean doesn't contain the obstacles in our crowded life of traffic and roads and people hastening about their business. To swim in the ocean is his for the asking, isn't that something, *señor*?'

'We had not thought——' Don Carlos smiled, but with a touch of sadness. 'Yes, my child, it is something but not everything. I have been very ambitious for my firstborn, Angela—has that been my sin, I wonder? The sin of pride?'

'You can be proud of all your children, *señor*.'

'*Si*, but Rique came first and he was everything a man hopes for in the son who will carry on the heritage, the courage, that dash of daring that induces Spaniards to face the great bulls in the arenas. *Macho*, my child. I have great fondness for Rique's brother, but he is of the artistic world and though I have never interfered in his life, I must confess that I find it strange a son of mine should have chosen the profession of film-making.'

'All the same, *señor*, Sebastian has proved himself a remarkable maker of films and he's thought very highly of in England. I enjoy a good film myself, and wouldn't you agree that there is less cruelty in a cinema film than in a bullring?'

'Ah, that British hatred of the bullfight!' The gleam of white teeth showed beneath the black moustache and into the Don's eyes came a smile that reminded

Angie so much of Rique; you are a woman, it seemed to say, but I am a man!

'The deer is still hunted in your country,' he mocked. 'What have you to say to that, eh?'

'Only that I hate it, *señor*.' Her grey-blue eyes reflected her intense loathing for those who used animals, and people, for their sport. 'It's a difficult world to live in, I'm afraid, for people who realise that all creatures have feelings and I only hope that those who inflict pain are going to find themselves in hell when the time comes.'

'So Maya and I did right to send for you,' Don Carlos said reflectively. 'You are *buen angel*, which we Spanish use to describe a tender-hearted person who is *simpática*. Of course you know our language, and you were brought up a Catholic like my own children. You abide by its tenets?'

'Not strictly,' Angie confessed. 'Nursing is such a demanding job, especially when a nurse does hospital work, so I just hope that the job itself supplements my lapses when I don't attend Mass or go to confession.'

'I am sure,' a glint of humour showed in the Don's dark eyes, 'that you have few sins to confess, is that not so, Angela?'

'I hope so, *señor*, but I don't think I live up to my name entirely. I'd hate to be a prig.'

'I have an idea Rique would hate it as well, you agree?'

'*Conforme*,' she said with feeling.

For several intent moments Don Carlos held Angie's grey-blue gaze, which under the big chandeliers of the hall had a luminosity that was shared by her fairness of

skin and hair. She looked young, untouched, slim to
delicacy in contrast to the Latin virility of Carlos de
Zaldo. It was this in her which he seemed to be study-
ing, as if it intrigued him, a man whose position in life
threw him too much in contact with people veneered
by politics, commerce and travel.

'Let me show you something.' He took her by the
hand and led her across the hall to where a large
colourful tapestry hung against the panelling. It had
been carefully repaired here and there, showing a lus-
trous design of a mythical dragon and a unicorn, and a
white-skinned girl tied to a tree, a wreath of red
berries on her long fair hair.

'I acquired this lovely thing about a year ago.' Don
Carlos peered curiously at the tied figure of the girl.
'She is threatened innocence, woman besieged by the
twin passions of desire and purity. The dragon is sym-
bolic of desire, the unicorn of the dream lover who remains always out of reach. I purchased the tapestry
because of its theme and because I thought it would
look striking in this position—what do you think of it?'

'It's fascinating, *señor*.' Angie gave him a quick look
and wondered if he suspected that she had followed
her heart to Bayaltar. He was a shrewd man and a
subtle one, so was his object in explaining the tapestry
a hint that Rique was out of her reach? Don Carlos
was Spanish to the bone and also a man of wealth;
there was little doubt in Angie's mind that he would
want his eldest son to marry a Latin girl of his own
social standing.

Perhaps the Don already had someone in mind . . .
perhaps it was the sensuous Ysabel whom he had
reared and cosseted, so that even to this day the two

girls, his daughter and his ward, had a *dueña* in the shape of his widowed sister, Doña Francisca.

It might even be that with Rique facing an uncertain future, his father wanted to see him married as soon as possible so that if the outcome was ultimately a tragic one, he might acquire a grandson even if he must lose his son.

'Come, you must be feeling hungry after your journey.'

Don Carlos escorted Angie into the handsome, high ceilinged dining-room which hadn't changed a great deal since the last time she had dined here. The horse-shoe windows were immense and hung with a rich velvet that fell into elegant folds. There was a dark dignity to the furniture whose sheen caught the lustre of wall-lamps. The table was perfectly set with silver and crystal upon a lace cloth, gardenias were grouped at the centre, their dark-green leaves gleaming against the lace.

Angie's heart felt heavy when her gaze rested upon the empty chair which had always been Rique's.

Don Carlos caught her glance and spread his hands speakingly. 'Rique is a grown man,' he sighed. 'I cannot order him to come to the table as if he were a boy. It makes me grieve that he prefers to shut himself away from our company.'

'Rique was always self-willed.' It was Doña Francisca who spoke, after giving Angie a regal inclination of her well-groomed head; a woman very much aware of her brother's position as Governor of the island. 'Have you dealt with a patient like Rique before, Nurse Hart?'

Angie felt a chill little stab at Doña Francisca's

tone of voice. It was as if she were putting Angie in her place; as if she didn't think it altogether proper that Rique's nurse should dine with the family.

'No,' Angie shook out her linen napkin and spread it across her lap, 'not like Señor Rique. He isn't a stranger to me, so I can't be quite impersonal towards him. I of course remember him the way he was.'

'You consider my nephew greatly changed?'

'Of course she does!' It was Maya who spoke, her dark eyes dwelling upon her aunt in a rather resentful way. 'Imagine having your sight snuffed out by a bomb—do you think it would make you sweet and charming?'

Doña Francisca frowned at her niece, every inch the matriarch with her elaborate coiffure, her haughty features, the big mourning cameo she always wore at her throat in memory of her husband. The dark purple silk of her dress was of the best, and the heavy diamond rings on her fingers were evidence of her wealth. She didn't live at the Residencia as a dependent but had her own suite of rooms to which her own furniture from her house in Madrid had been shipped. She was the type of childless woman who had developed a severity towards the young rather than the inclination to indulge them.

'Rique chose a career in the army, Maya. He knew the risks involved; the kind of risks that would not have endangered him had he agreed to enter my late husband's law practice. Carlos will agree with me that Rique has the ability to use his mind, it runs in the blood, but——'

'Fighting also runs in the blood, *hermana mia*,' her brother intercepted.

'And look at the result!' she exclaimed. 'Blinded at his age, scarred, and turning into a morose recluse! Had he been a son of mine——'

'He's a son of mine,' Don Carlos said, a flare to his nostrils. 'I am very proud of Rique. He did his duty by Spain, and there remains a lot of hope that he will recover himself completely.'

'I pray for it,' she agreed. 'Each day I speak with *La Virgen* and ask that she bestow on him a *milagro*. He is your heir, Carlos. He should have considered that before marching off to get himself a medal!'

'Enough!' Don Carlos gave his sister a warning look. 'What is done is done, *destino*! Let us eat dinner!'

'As you say, brother, destiny, but it would be courteous on Rique's side to make the effort to come to the table. We understand his awkwardness and make allowances for it.'

'Angela must charm him into joining us,' Ysabel drawled. She was seated across the table from Angie and one of her restless, pampered hands was toying with a wine glass. 'Do you think you are going to manage him? As Tia says, he is very self-willed and can be as obstinate as a bull. Have you a firm enough hand, do you think?'

'We have a saying in England,' Angie rejoined, 'we don't run until we've learned to walk. My patient is blind and he lives for the time being in a different world from ours; a world of sounds and scents which he must learn to sort out, and of obstacles he might crash into. If you wish to discover Rique's world, then I suggest that you tie a scarf over your eyes and explore your own bedroom; the experience will be a frightening and a bewildering one. You'll no longer see the compass of walls and so your world will have become a larger one and you'll have the feeling that you might fall off the edge of it.'

Ysabel stared across at Angie, a gleam of hatred in her eyes. 'I see you have given a lot of thought to—Rique. Have you experimented with a scarf over your eyes?'

'Yes,' Angie said simply. 'I forced myself to spend several hours in total darkness; even so I had in my mind the knowledge that I could remove the scarf and see the light. Rique can't do that. He has to adjust his mind to the fact that the light has gone out, and because he has been a man of action the adjustment is a frustrating one.'

'If I were Rique——' his sister gave a choked sound, 'I—I'd want to hide away with my pain and fear——'

'Rique isn't going to be encouraged by me to hide himself away,' Angie said gently. 'He must be taught to accept his blindness as a challenge—a battle. He joined the army because it offered him those two things, and once he accepts that his darkness can be conquered, then he'll conquer it.'

'You truly believe he will put up a fight, Angie?' Tears glimmered in Maya's eyes. 'I loved seeing him in his uniform, it suited him so well! I keep remembering the time he was home on leave when we went out to dinner at the Castelo de Madrigal, when I introduced him to Roddy——' She broke off and dropped her gaze to her soup; her shoulders drooped and Angie saw a tear fall from her cheek.

'I can't bear it,' Maya choked, 'the way life can be so happy, and then out of the blue an awful dark cloud falls over everything. I—I keep waiting for the next horrible thing to happen—as if we're cursed!'

'Enough!' Don Carlos brought his fist down on the table, rattling the china and glassware. 'I forbid you to talk in such a way! Come, *mia* Maya, eat your dinner and try to cast such thoughts out of your mind. Forget that guitar-strumming young man. He is not for you! I have said so and you must accept my word!'

'I'm not a child any more,' she protested.

'I have ordered you to forget him.' Carlos de Zaldo looked adamant. 'We are a good Catholic family and we have always lived by the Church's doctrines, and I tell you again, girl, that I will not permit into this household a young man who has been divorced.'

'You wouldn't have known about it,' Maya said heatedly, 'if Ysabel hadn't told you. She delights in carrying tales to you!'

'I appreciate that Ysabel had the good sense to tell me.' His eyes glittered across the gardenias at his daughter, and Angie noticed yet again the likeness between Don Carlos and Rique. Not only was it physical but both of them had a kind of arrogance when it came to making a judgement, upon which they took a stand as firm as iron. So Maya's plight was explained; the young man she had fallen for had broken a Catholic commandment by getting divorced. No wonder she had tried to keep it a secret from her father . . . the kind of skeleton in the closet which Ysabel would release with relish.

Angie saw that she sat there smiling her cat's smile while the bones were aired.

'Roddy wasn't to blame for the divorce,' Maya argued. 'His wife fell in love with someone in another singing group——'

'Singers!' Her father's lip curled beneath his black moustache and he had a dangerous look. 'They think nothing of carrying on with each other!'

'You're so Latin and prejudiced, Papa.' Maya's dark eyes held a flash of fire. 'You rule my life a-and want to ruin it, yet it's well known that you fell in love at first sight!'

'Your mother was an angel, unlike this strumming pretty boy who parades about on a stage, making noises on an instrument that Spaniards *can* play.' The chandelier above the table gleamed in the blade of the knife with which the Don carved thick slices from a roasted leg of lamb, laying the slices on plates that the maid handed around.

'How can you say, Maya, that this young man fell in love with you at first sight?' her father pursued. 'He has already had a wife and one presumes that he was in love with her when they married.'

'The marriage was a mistake——' Maya's plate trembled in her hand as she took it. 'People are only human, a-and she was older than Roddy and she seduced him.'

'Naturally he would say so, and a carefully reared girl like you would be bound to believe him. I assure you, *querida*, you will soon recover your good senses and realise your folly. You are my flesh and blood, *mia* Maya, and it is my cherished wish that you make a sound and happy alliance with a young man of Spanish blood and principles.'

'Like the son of one of your *compadres*?' she flared.

'You could do worse,' his gaze held hers, 'and you very nearly did.'

Maya gave him a baleful look, while Ysabel took dainty bites of food and sensuous sips of wine, a full-bodied island wine that glimmered deep ruby in the stemmed glasses.

Angie could feel its warmth stealing through her own veins, but at heart she remained sad and troubled. The old sunlit days of summer had got lost in shadows; playtime was over, as Rique had said, and adulthood had brought its problems and pains down on their heads. Her gaze dwelt on Maya, who was picking at the delicious food in a sulky way. Angie knew that Maya had always been an obedient daughter, so she wouldn't be likely to actively oppose her father's wishes, but his adamant disapproval of the young entertainer had obviously upset her, and added on to this was her concern for her blinded brother.

The meal proceeded to the sweet course, vanilla ice-cream doused in hot black cherries which had been simmered in a liqueur. It had been a favourite sweet of the Don's children, but because the two boys weren't at the table tonight, demanding second helpings, Angie found less pleasure in it.

The sweetness had gone out of it, and at the close of the meal Maya refused coffee in the *sala* and said she was going for a walk. Her father didn't argue with her but tugged thoughtfully at his moustache. 'I have more trouble with my children now they are grown up than I had when they were at school. How do I make Maya understand that I am firm with her for her sake?'

'Is it for her sake, *señor*?' Angie had asked the question before she could stop herself. 'What I mean is, shouldn't everyone be allowed to make their own mistakes?'

He gazed at her with a frown joining the dark brows above his bold nose, and he looked so like Rique when his opinion was questioned.

'Are you saying that I am being too harsh with my own daughter?' he demanded. 'You think I should allow her to see this young man who has divorced one woman and who makes a precarious living as an entertainer? *Dios*, I could be failing in my duty as a parent if I allowed myself to be moved by her tears. Her life has been a sheltered one and she is still very young emotionally. She has been struck by calf love and will soon be over the worst of it.'

'She seems so unhappy—*gracias*.' Angie accepted black coffee laced with Spanish cognac and settled back into one of the big deep-cushioned chairs that gave the *sala* such a comfortable look. The furniture was richly carved in the Spanish way, there were cabinets mullioned with antique glass where the Don's collection of jade and ivory was housed. Beyond the range of horseshoe windows lay the night-enshrouded garden, where jasmine vines were laden with small white flowers; star jasmines which grew and clung to elderly trees, draping the twisted limbs as if to hide their age and lend them grace. The jasmine, Angie remembered, was all over the garden like lace.

Ysabel had gone to the piano, whose ivory keys had gone honey with age. She ran her fingers along them and produced a thread of tune which Angie recognised.

It was a French song they used to chant as teenagers who didn't fully realise the meaning in the words, nor the significance they might have as each one of them grew older and wiser.

> '*Plaisir d'amour ne dure qu'un moment,*
> *Chagrin d'amour dure toute la vie.*'

'The joys of love last but a moment.' Don Carlos

murmured the words as he sat down in a large winged chair and studied the cognac he had poured into a cut-glass inhaler. 'The pains of love last your whole life through.'

He moved the inhaler back and forth and breathed the aroma of the cognac up into his nostrils. '*Ay*, it can be that way for some people, but I would not want it to be that way for Maya—nor other of my children.'

He raised the inhaler and drank slowly from it, savouring the contents with the ease of the worldly man. His gaze dwelt upon Angie, who sat among the cushions of her chair and yet whose body was tense and unrelaxed. Her heart gave a nervous throb and she wondered what Rique's father was sifting through his mind. Had her readiness to come and nurse his son awoken a suspicion that she had fallen victim to a love that could provide more pain than joy?

'This is an old ripe brandy that was put down in the cellars in my father's time,' he remarked. 'Instead of this and the return of her friend my lovelorn daughter prefers to walk alone. The folly of youth that like this brandy has to mature in order to arrive at its best time of life.'

'Brandy which we are now consuming, *señor*,' Angie was so bold as to remind him.

A glint came into his eyes and his lip twitched the black moustache. 'Are you going to be quietly abrasive towards my son, and is he going to take it, I wonder? What so far has been his reaction?'

'At present, *señor*, he'd like to mount my head on a spear.'

'Ah, that terrible?'

Angie smiled slightly and as she sipped her coffee

she observed Don Carlos through her lashes, the long dark lashes that so often shielded blue or grey eyes; nature's protection from the sun but handy for secret observations.

The *hidalgo*'s every feature was carved from his Castilian heritage; he had the inborn look of privilege and power, but he was no despot who ruled with a rod of iron. He had enormous charm and he used it, sometimes quite deliberately in the interests of the islanders. He safeguarded their tourist trade and protected their commerce just as if they were part of his own family. He was a throwback to the lords of old but without the cruel streak in his arrogance.

Black sapphires gleamed at his impeccable cuffs as he selected a cigar from a copper-trimmed teakwood box on a carved table beside his chair, and Angie felt a stirring of interest in him that was very different from her schoolgirlish memory of him. She had grown up, but he in the way of the Latin male had remained very vital and showed his age only in the way his hair had gone from black to iron-grey.

In that moment Doña Francisca entered the room. She had been upstairs to fetch her embroidery; she could have sent the maid for it, but Angie suspected that she had called in on Rique. If she had hoped to persuade him to come downstairs it appeared that she had been unsuccessful.

The Don rose from his chair to attend to his sister's drinking requirements and Angie caught her breath at his height and distinction. So would Rique look in middle-age . . . if Rique should live.

'*Gracias,* Carlos.' Doña Francisca accepted her glass of cognac and placed it on the table at her side. She opened her work-basket and took a filmy object from

it. As her brother returned to his chair and his cigar,
his sister's dark eyes settled upon Angie.

No one spoke; only the tinkling of the piano keys
filled the room, along with the pleasant drift of
Havana cigar smoke.

'I have here,' Doña Francisca said at last, 'a chalice
veil which has been in our family a long time—it may
be only a superstition but such veils are believed to
soothe and perhaps heal a person who has suffered a
bad injury. I am going to confess, Nurse Hart, that
several times I have tried to persuade my nephew to
allow me to place this chalice veil over his face, but he
refuses me. He laughs at the mere suggestion.'

'So he should,' Don Carlos broke in. 'It is necro-
mancy!'

'You and Rique,' his sister exclaimed, '*cinicos!*'

'Merciful powers of heaven, *hermana*, we aren't
living in the Dark Ages! Rique hasn't an outbreak of
warts that raw meat and a wedding ring are going to
magic away. Women!'

'Quite so, Carlos *mio*, and where would you men be
without them? Come, there is nothing to be lost, and
the veil, remember, has been blessed.'

'How a member of this family came by it is a matter
of conjecture.' He flicked ash impatiently from his
cigar. 'You do realise that it isn't quite in order for
such an article to be in your hands? I trust you are
aware that certain members of our ancestry were a
trifle on the shady side?'

'That was many years ago, brother, and they were
conquistadores.' His sister spoke soothingly. 'I have
proof that the veil has certain powers—take the case of
my maid Pilar and those pains in her back. I swathed

her loins in the veil and the pains receded. Then there was my sister-in-law's daughter with her tendency to miscarry—again the veil was used and the next thing you know Alida gives birth to twins. I tell you, twins!'

'A miracle,' her brother responded, looking sardonic through the smoke of his cigar. 'A mere case of nature making up for what had been lost—nature has a way of doing that.'

Angie listened to the exchange and decided that a little diplomacy was required; older Spanish women were often superstitious and it also showed that Doña Francisca was very concerned about Rique, something which was bound to appeal to Angie.

'Doña Francisca,' she spoke gently, 'would you like me to have a try at laying the chalice veil on your nephew?'

His aunt clenched her hands in the filmy veil. 'It could work, could it not, but he won't allow me near him with it. I tried and he flung it to the floor.'

'Proof of his good sense,' Don Carlos growled.

'Right now Rique is snarling like a tiger in a net,' Angie pointed out, 'and the veil touching his skin would have that feel.'

The Don's sister gazed at Angie with a dawning respect in her eyes.'You seem so young, and yet you understand——'

'I understand, *señora*, that someone's faith and hope can add that extra ingredient which inspires a patient to get well. You realise that Rique's hearing has become very acute—I'll cover his pillow with the veil and he'll then sleep with his head against it.'

'You are going along with this nonsense?' Don Carlos exclaimed.

Angie gave him a steady look and allowed him to read her eyes. He had to understand that beneath her somewhat sharp manner his sister was greatly concerned for Rique. 'Where is the harm, *señor*?' she murmured.

Smoke eddied from his lips as he probed her grey-blue eyes with his dark gaze. 'Women!' His moustache twitched. 'What strange creatures you are—well, don't blame me if Rique rips the veil to pieces.'

'You will permit, Carlos?' His sister beamed at him.

'If you must play your games of magic.' He rested his head against the back of his chair. 'What do you think of the matter, Ysabel?'

She strolled to his chair and sank down gracefully on a footstool, the skirt of deep-green velvet pooling around her; she gazed up at him and there was something about her pose and her eyes that put Angie in mind of the Siamese cat El Greco had painted . . . a kind of slumbering self-satisfaction that concealed claws.

'I had no idea that nurses dealt in black magic,' she murmured. 'Does it distress you, Angela, seeing Rique deprived of his *machismo*?'

'I don't imagine for one moment that Rique has lost that ingredient.' Angie studied the Don's ward with uneasy curiosity; with her long neck and the animal sheen of her eyes she attracted and yet repelled. 'He has to learn to live in a way we can't even imagine and when he discovers that he has powers beyond ours, then he'll be in full command of himself again.'

'To hear you speak, Angela, one would think that you knew him—dare I say intimately?' Ysabel's eyes probed Angie with a suspicion that made her nerves crawl.

'I've been a nurse for almost five years.' Angie re-joined. 'I know that courage and will-power can work wonders. If I wasn't confident of my ability to help Rique then I wouldn't be here.'

'Oh, come,' Ysabel gave a scoffing laugh, 'I be-lieve you would have crawled on your hands and knees to be at his side.'

'Ysabel!' The Don's dark brows meshed in a frown. 'What in the name of the devil are you saying?'

'Angela knows what I'm saying,' she replied. 'Ask her.'

Don Carlos stared at his ward, then abruptly his gaze was fastened upon Angie, who went hot and cold, as if her charming host had suddenly become her in-quisitor.

CHAPTER FOUR

ANGIE had never been placed in such an awkward situation, and distrust of Ysabel turned to dislike. Ysabel had let suspicion glide into the *sala* like a snake and it hung there, weaving invisibly back and forth as Don Carlos searched Angie's face.

She was to nurse his son and he was a man of stern dictates where morals were concerned. She would be sleeping in the room adjoining Rique's and often she would be in and out of his bedroom. Now because of Ysabel's remark there was a question mark in the Don's eyes; she knew he was asking himself if he had done right to invite a young nurse into his home to take care of his son.

His eyes went all over Angie as she sat there in her wine dress against the creamy brocade of her chair, her fair hair spilling into her wide eyes, their pupils darkly expanded against the grey-blue.

'This room is like a tomb!' A cane struck the door frame and Angie turned instantly to look; her heart lurched when she saw Rique looming in the doorway, his cane poised in his hand as if it were a rapier.

'My boy,' Don Carlos rose to his feet, 'come in at once and take a drink with us.'

'Have you been sitting in here playing statues?' Rique probed the air with his cane as he advanced into the *sala*.

Angie watched him and wanted to warn him to be careful of the furniture, but a band of constraint seemed locked about her throat since Ysabel's insinuation.

'*Cuidado*!' But even as the Don spoke his warning, Rique blundered into an occasional table with carved edges, striking his shinbones and stumbling with a curse.

'The hell with it!' He thrashed out with his cane even as Angie, driven to her feet, made an attempt to guide him to a chair. The cane struck her across the arm and she couldn't quite strangle a cry as the blow stung her bare skin.

'*Dios*, who have I struck?'

Angie rubbed her stinging arm and heard Ysabel laugh quietly to herself. 'Only me,' she said.

'Only you, eh?' He stood above her looking grim and lost. 'Are you badly wounded?'

'I'll survive, *amigo*.'

'Has it taught you not to be an angel who rushes in where others fear to tread?'

'Not really.'

'Brave words, Angel.' His tone of voice was deeply sardonic. 'I bet I could make a coward of you.'

'Are you threatening to put a grass snake in my bed?' she asked. 'You did that to me when we were teenagers.'

'Now we're all grown up, eh, and I must think of something a little more alarming to put in your bed. I wonder what would alarm you most—a man, perhaps?'

She caught her breath and knew he heard her because of the rather cruel little smile that curled his lips.

'A touch of the cane wouldn't hurt you,' she said.

'Am I being a naughty boy, nurse?'

'I think you're determined not to make my job an easy one.'

'You knew it would be no bed of roses taking me on, Angel. You chose to come here, I didn't ask for you. You're the very last person I wanted around. Ask my father; he'll tell you what my reaction was when I was told you were coming from England.'

Angie glanced at Don Carlos before she could stop herself; he spread his hands speakingly. 'I assure you it was nothing personal, Angela . . . in his present frame of mind Rique would resent Florence Nightingale.'

'Padre, there is no need to spare her feelings.' Rique spoke callously. 'I didn't want her anywhere near me—do you think I'd tolerate a slip of a girl in charge of me if I had half an eye to see with?'

'I'm a trained nurse and I'm not afraid to take you on,' Angie said heatedly. Anger and hurt simmered together inside her; he was being deliberately boorish towards her in front of his father and only by walking out of this house would she protect herself from the cuts that seemed to draw blood from her heart. She didn't like to think of the state her emotions would be in by the time this job was over, and come what may she was going through with it . . . it somehow seemed her fate to do so.

'I'll have you polite to Angela.' Don Carlos spoke with a touch of anger. 'It's kind of her to come and take on no easy task. You are my son, Rique, and I know you in my flesh and bones; I know that if it suits you to give a woman hell, you will do so without mercy.'

'Are you listening to my father, Angel?' Rique turned his head, seeking her with his blind eyes. 'Expect no mercy if you take me on.'

'I'm not a quitter,' she rejoined. 'You should meet some of the Matrons I've worked under.'

'Dragons spitting fire, eh?' Suddenly his face was drawn and he glanced about him blindly. 'Will someone give me a drink? I'm bored by all this talk of bravery—I'm the proof of the sort of rewards it collects! It either tears you apart, or puts out every damn light in the world!'

'Come,' Don Carlos eased his son into a chair and placed a glass in his hand. 'I will pour you a good measure of cognac and you will try to be civilised, no?'

'No one can afford to be civilised any more.' Rique gazed broodingly into the void whose darkness made Angie tremble for him. 'The world has gone mad; the devil has been let loose and he's stirring up a fire that may consume all of us one of these days.'

'Rique *mio*,' his aunt leaned from her couch and pressed his knee, 'forget about war. You are home and safe with us, here on our beautiful island far from it all. All that is asked of you now, *querido*, is that you get well and strong again.'

'Your aunt speaks good sense, Rique.' His father poured a generous measure of cognac into this glass. 'The devil has always been among us and we continue to fight him. We are proud of you, *mi hijo*. You wore you uniform with pride and courage.'

'Pride comes before a fall.' Rique tossed back most of his drink, undiluted and dark-gold in the glass. 'Perhaps with any luck I shall fall and break my neck one of these days. Anything would be better than this—this infernal darkness!'

Abruptly he gave a harsh, jeering laugh. 'Is my angel of mercy giving me a look of shocked reproof? Somehow I sense that she is.'

'How astute you are, Rique!' It was Ysabel who answered him. 'You are so quick at picking up vibrations.'

'Training for undercover work does it, *cara*.' He moved the brandy snifter beneath his nose. 'Is Maya in the room—she's being very quiet if she is?'

'Your sister has gone walking.' Don Carlos was looking directly at his son and Angie saw a look of grave sadness on his face. 'She considers herself heartbroken because I find unacceptable this young singer she has become infatuated with. If a man will divorce one woman, then he will divorce two—it becomes a habit! The alliance is out of the question!'

'Perhaps, Padre, you are being too much the traditional Spaniard.' Rique murmured. 'What is divorce when people are tearing other people apart with bombs?'

Angie winced as she felt a shadow of his pain, his never-to-be-forgotten memory of the burning, blinding, flesh-tearing impact of the bomb which had injured him; still in his mind he must hear the screams of a dying comrade.

She wondered if he had nightmares when he did sleep at night.

'I know what is best for Maya.' Don Carlos spoke firmly. 'She has had security in her home, and she must have security in her marriage.'

'She might wish to have some adventure,' Rique suggested.

'Travel, certainly,' his father agreed, 'with the right man.'

'The right man for her, Padre, might not be the right man for you.'

Don Carlos frowned. 'Are you taking me to task, Rique?'

'No, I'm merely expressing an opinion. Love can hurt, if it's love she feels for this boy.'

'Calf love!' Don Carlos arose and added cognac to his son's glass. 'Most girls and young men go through it; it is youth flexing its muscles for the real encounter. When that moment comes—I tell you, *hijo*, were Maya really in love with the singer, then she would defy me and not argue with me. She would elope with him!'

'She may be doing that right now.' Rique's lip twitched as he put the brandy glass to his mouth.

'*Por infierno!*' The Don's eyes flashed. 'She would not sit down on her bottom for a week!'

'Always supposing you caught up with her and her boy-friend.' Rique was openly smiling, leading his father on, and it was a sight that warmed Angie. For a few moments he had forgotten himself, and she promised herself she'd hang out a flag the day he forgot himself for an hour! That was the way this battle was going to be won, inch by inch as men on a battlefield wormed their way towards the enemy until they reared up to confront the black shape face to face.

'I'd make sure the pair of them didn't get off this island,' the Don said aggressively. 'I will not have my daughter marrying that—that infidel! She knows it, too. Maya knows I'm to be obeyed in this matter.'

'Padre,' Rique laughed softly, 'you never cease to be Spanish. You lavish great affection upon Maya and in a sense you do this so she will marry the man of your choice.'

'*Ay*, and you will do the same, *hijo*, with your children.'

'My children!' Instantly the hard cold mask was back upon Rique's face and his eyes were as blind as stones. 'You will have to look to Seb for your grandchildren——'

He broke off with a sigh and Angie rose from her chair and went to him; gently she laid a hand upon his shoulder. 'It's time you were in bed,' she said.

Instantly there was tension in the muscles of his shoulder, then he shrugged and climbed to his feet until he towered above her. She wasn't a short girl, but the top of her head came only to the level of his hard obstinate chin.

'Are you going to tuck me up and hold my hand until I go to sleep?' he asked quizzically.

Ysabel gave a slightly edged laugh. 'Is that all you require these nights to send you off to sleep, Rique?'

He glanced in the direction of Ysabel's voice and even though his gaze was blind Ysabel seemed to accentuate her languorous pose against the window frame, where the rich sweep of the curtains seemed to enhance her exotic looks.

'The strange thing is,' he chose to ignore the innuendo in her remark and spoke seriously, 'that when you can't tell night from day you seem to feel less inclined to sleep. I suppose daylight tires the eyes to a certain extent, but it's a trial I'd welcome with open arms.'

'*Mi hijo*——' the Don's face twisted into a grimace of love and pain, 'it will happen, you will see!'

'In my infrequent dreams?' The cynicism in Rique's voice was total in that moment. 'Don't you think I asked for the verdict when they removed the bandages and examined my eyes? I insisted upon knowing, though I knew already that there was no light perception. *Dios*, don't think I'm accepting it,' his lip snarled. 'I'm only human. I want to do my share of living and loving, but not like this!'

'Rique——' The cry was wrung from Don Carlos, then he glanced in a kind of anguish at Angie, as if she might have the formula to ease the harsh pain that linked father and son and yet left them with an abyss between them . . . that abyss of darkness the sighted could only imagine.

'Rique, *mi hijo*, if I could give you my eyes!' The words seemed to come from the Don's heart itself.

'Padre, you never said a kinder thing.' Rique smiled, but his eyes were empty. 'You must forgive me for being blunt, but I can't live on lies, even those meant kindly. Let it be understood from this moment onward, I am blind. The lights aren't just dim, they are out.'

At these words a sob caught in Doña Francisca's

throat and dragging a lace handkerchief from her sleeve she buried her face in it.

'Tia, don't.' He had guessed that it was his aunt who had broken down in tears. 'Remember what you said to me when I came home, I chose to go where the wars were going on. I have always chosen my way, and I always shall, so please wipe your eyes.'

'Rique, I am going to escort you to your—room.' Ysabel, with not even a hint of tears in her eyes, strolled to Rique and tucked her arm through his. As she did this she looked at Angie and there were glints of insolence in her eyes. *What does he want with a nurse?* she seemed to be saying. *What this man needs is a woman.*

'*Buenas noches,*' he said, and went with Ysabel from the *sala*, leaving Angie with the helpless feeling that she might as well have stayed in England with her memories of Rique. He didn't want her with him, not Rique the man. It was only his bodily hurts that required her kind of attention . . . his physical passions as they returned would be dealt with by other women.

Ysabel, for example, whom he remembered as a woman and not as a schoolgirl in plaits and bare feet crusted with the sands of the Bayaltar beach.

She gave a start as her hands were taken into those of Don Carlos. He looked down into her eyes for a long moment. 'Bear with him, Angela, for my sake.'

'For your sake, *señor?*'

'Mine.' He raised her hands and brushed them with his lips. 'Now go to your bed, you have had a long day. Leave Ysabel to deal with him tonight.'

'Very well, *señor.*' Angie didn't dare to question what he meant by his words, but they seemed to underline what she had thought earlier, that it would suit Don Carlos to arrange a marriage between his son and his ward.

'Goodnight,' she murmured.

'*Buenas noches*, my child. Have good repose.'

She nodded and left the *sala* with the feeling that repose was the last thing she would enjoy this first night at the Residencia as Rique de Zaldo's nurse. When she reached the *galeria* it surprised her to see Ysabel coming away from Rique's door, her face a tight-lipped mask. She swept past Angie without a word, and when Angie reached Rique's door it was standing ajar and she saw him standing with his head bowed and his hands clenched as if he wanted to swing a fist at the blackness all around him, as if hoping he might punch a hole in it and let in the light.

Angie stood hesitant, then walked into the room. She trod carpet, but he must have caught the rustle of her dress. 'Go away, Ysabel,' he said. 'Go to someone who can tell you how seductive you are.'

'It's me,' Angie said.

'So, are you going to undress me and put me to bed?' As he spoke he yanked open his tie and dropped it to the floor. He unbuttoned his shirt to his belt, unlatched it and stepped out of his trousers.

Quite coolly Angie fetched his pyjamas. 'Put those on,' she ordered.

'You sound like a drill sergeant, do you know that?' The raking hardness of his legs straddled the carpet. 'Is that your intention, to drill me into an obedient robot, tapping my way about the island and doing my little tricks for the onlookers? Is that on the agenda, nurse? You plan to be my sweet persuader?'

'I plan to persuade you to rejoin the human race,' she agreed, 'but you don't make me feel very sweet about the prospect. There are doctors who have sarcastic tongues, but yours could take first prize.'

'I'm glad I could still take a prize for something.' He knotted the cord of his pyjama trousers and stood in front of her bare-chested. The hair on his chest was dark as that on his head and it was shaped into the form of a crucifix. A jagged piece of metal had left a raw-looking scar halfway down his left side and the look of it made Angie wince. If Rique was sore and abrasive, then he certainly had reason to be so. But common sense told her that she would be doing him no favours if she encouraged him to feel sorry for himself.

'I don't relish the idea of being your nurse, Rique. You were always rather arrogant and sure of your place in the world.'

'And now I've been taken down a peg or two, eh?' Swiftly his hand shot out and as if there was radar in his fingertips they found her and jerked her towards him. Angie didn't struggle; his muscular capacity was far in excess of hers and she feigned indifference to the warm hardness of his chest against her. It wasn't easy to pretend indifference when all she was aware of in the world was Rique's lean, scarred face and his bare shoulders looming over her.

'As if I—I'd think such an awful thing!' she reproved him.

'I'd prefer it to pity for Maya's poor benighted brother who used to pull your hair and put grass snakes in your bed.' Suddenly his arm snaked around her and he held her hurtfully close to him. 'Did you imagine I'd be easy to handle because I'm blind?'

'Did you imagine, Rique, that blindness would make you less of a man?'

His muscles pressed into her and she felt a quiver go through him. 'Who gave you the right to dissect my thoughts and feelings? Take some advice and don't go probing into my mind—you might discover things that you won't like.'

'As I've said before, *amigo*, I'm not a schoolgirl any longer.' Through the silky fabric of her dress she could feel the thud of his heart; the skin of his shoulders was smooth and tawny-brown, and nerves twisted deep inside her as she felt a surging urge to press her lips to his skin. What would he do if she gave way to the dangerous impulse? Would he thrust her away from him, or would he throw her down on his bed and let loose his rage upon her?

Angie felt a fluid weakness in her knees; never before had she let her thoughts be so uncaged. She shivered as his fingers stroked the side of her neck.

'Your skin is soft as silk—go to hell, Angel!' He thrust her angrily away from him. 'You're a little chit who dares to think that with a little help from her vast store of worldly knowledge she can help me come to terms with this hellish black hole I live in!'

He stared ahead of him into the blackness and his mouth twisted. 'You feel and sound and act like a schoolgirl. Your fetching nurse's uniform will be lost on me, Angel. Your good intentions aren't what I need.'

'What do you need, Rique?' she asked quietly.

'You really want to know, *chiquita*?'

'Yes. I shall try not to faint with shock.'

His lips twitched as if with a faint stirring of amusement. 'I want a bad woman and a loaded gun, nurse, in that order. Bring me those and you'll be doing me the only favour worth your while.'

'I'll bring you hot chocolate with cinnamon added.'

His words had made her wince, half shocked. 'How do you sleep?'

'With difficulty.' He dragged a hand across his brow as if it ached. 'With my eyes open or shut I see the same nightmare. It begins with a bomb striking the wall near my head and it ends with a bloody blown-off hand striking me across the face. Is that enough for one session, or do you fancy a few more grisly details?'

'Climb into bed, Rique, and I'll fetch your drink——'

'Make it a malt whisky and you have a deal.'

'You've had enough to drink for one night.' She turned back the covers of his bed and plumped his pillows. She saw a box of *cigarros* on his night table along with a lighter, a clock with prominent numerals so he could read the time, several unopened letters and a pillbox.

'Why haven't you asked somebody to read your letters to you?' she asked.

'They aren't important,' he shrugged, 'not any more.'

Which answer seemed to indicate to Angie that they were probably from a woman. Angie picked them up and studied the handwriting on the envelopes. Three were addressed in a feminine hand, but the fourth was in a sprawling, dark-inked script, the stamps slapped on the envelope at an angle.

'I think one of these is from a man,' she said. 'Perhaps an army buddy of yours. I'll read it to you when I've brought your hot drink.'

He stood frowning in the direction of her voice. 'I don't think I want you to bother,' he decided. 'Toss the letters into a drawer.'

Angie obeyed his wish regarding three of the letters, but placed the fourth near his clock. She picked up the pillbox and opened it; inside were a number of small round pills which she guessed were to alleviate his headaches and help him to sleep.

'Aren't you going to put your pyjama jacket on?' she asked.

'I get too hot.' He quirked an eyebrow and the edge of his lip. 'I usually sleep in my skin, but I'm taking your modesty into consideration.'

'A nurse gets to see a lot of funny sights, so don't mind me.' She walked to the door. 'I shan't be long. If you're asleep when I return, than I shan't disturb you.'

His hand was feeling along the pillows as he gauged his way into bed. 'Make it a whisky and I promise to stay awake—so you can kiss me goodnight.'

'You've had your quota of drink for tonight,' she rejoined, thinking how dark and big he looked against the white linen of his pillows and sheets. 'It could be too much of that that makes you have nightmares.'

'So like some big kid I'm going to be forced to drink hot chocolate.'

'With cinnamon.' A smile glimmered in her eyes as she closed his door behind her and made her way downstairs to the kitchen. How well she remembered the big, scrubbed, aromatic kitchen, with its range of deep cupboards housing all sorts of pickles, preserves and pâtés. Jars of cherries in wine, plums in a deep red juice, peaches and apricots that went into the delicious pies.

Angie stood gazing around her as she waited for milk to warm in the saucepan; the memories came sift-

ing back, one upon another like the sweet fitful tune
from a music-box. Echoes of more carefree days came
drifting into the kitchen, when they would crowd in
here after hours on the beach, demanding slices of pie
and glasses of lemonade. Rique, being the eldest,
would lounge on a corner of the big scrubbed table and
drink *sangria* with an amused smile in his mica-gray
eyes, their depth intensified by his black lashes and
slightly peaked brows.

'Children, the lot of them,' his expression seemed to
say, and Angie breathed a sigh as she mixed chocolate
into the milk and added a dash of cinnamon and sugar.
She found some biscuits in a tin and laid a few on a
plate, then carrying the steaming chocolate and biscuits on a tray she went upstairs again, taking the rear
stairs to the *galeria* in order to avoid running into
someone.

It was somehow private, even something of a luxury,
to be able to take Rique a late-night snack. She had
access to his bedside because she was his nurse, and
with the door closed behind her and shaded light spilling warmly on to the bed, the man in it seemed to
belong solely to her for a short while.

He accepted the drink without comment, and perch-
ing herself on the foot of his bed Angie opened the
letter with the masculine writing on the envelope.

Rique's sharp ears caught the rustle of notepaper. 'I
thought I told you to toss those letters into a drawer,
you little snooper.'

'Ignoring people's letters is rude,' she rejoined. 'I'm
not reading the ones from your lady friend, so relax;
this letter is from a man named Torcal——'

'Torcal de Byas!' he exclaimed.

'Shall I read you what he says?'

Rique crunched a biscuit, his brows drawn together. 'We were in hospital at the same time.'

'So I gather from his letter.' Without further ado Angie began to read aloud what this man with the unusual name had to say. He was now on his feet, he wrote, and wondered if he would be permitted to visit Rique at the Residencia if he came to Bayaltar to stay a while. They had, he went on, been through a similar experience in that their mutual lives had been disrupted by dire injury and it sometimes helped to share the fears and hopes of men facing the future with a disability.

Angie carefully folded the letter and studied Rique's brooding expression. 'He sounds a nice person,' she commented. 'Was he very badly hurt?'

Rique inclined his head. 'Grenade impact . . . it castrated him!'

'Oh—dear lord!' Angie was a nurse, but she blanched at the stark words and the distressing image they evoked. 'Why—why do people have to do such cruel things to each other? Why does there have to be hate in the world?'

'Because the devil put it there! I'm not a philosopher, Angel, I know only that evil stalks among us and some of us are foolish enough to go out and try to slay the dragons. For much of the time the warriors keep their weapons clean and their brass polished and they try not to mind when kids in back streets hurl dirty names at them. Soldiering isn't unlike nursing, when you come to think of it. Much of it is tied up with discipline and duty . . . and it's grossly underpaid. Makes you wonder why we do it, eh?'

Angie pressed a hand to the sigh on her lips. Rique would soldier no more; all the strength and spirit in him were going to be needed to fight a different kind of battle.

'This letter should be answered,' she said carefully. 'If you dictate your answer tomorrow, I'll post it for you.'

'No,' he shook his head, 'if I don't reply, then Byas won't come to Bayaltar.'

'Why shouldn't he come, *amigo*? He's reaching out a hand to a friend——'

'*Dios*, I'm a fine one for him to reach out to—talk about the blind leading the crippled! Are you suggesting we weep on each other's shoulder for what we have mutually lost—my sight—his manhood?'

Angie flinched and watched him seeking on the night table for his *cigarros* and forced herself not to help him. He fumbled a *cigarro* out of the box and placed it between his lips, then he went searching for the lighter and this time Angie picked it up and flicked the flame for him. He sucked it to the tip of the dark-leafed *cigarro* and his eyes seemed to fix themselves upon her face.

'Crying never hurt anyone,' she said, as she snapped the flame back into the gold cylinder. 'Unless you consider yourself too *macho* for tears?'

'Step a little nearer to this bed, nurse, and I'll prove my *machoism*—you did say, didn't you, that being blind didn't make me less of a man?' Abruptly he frowned and his nostrils emitted a stream of strong smoke. 'So you advise me to answer Torcal's letter, eh?'

'It would be the kind thing to do, *amigo*.'

'It might not be the wisest, Angel. You might find yourself with two lost souls on your hands.'

'I expect I should cope. I wouldn't be a very good nurse if I didn't want to help people—not that I'm being self-righteous.'

'God forbid me a nurse with too much virtue!' A cynical smile twisted the edge of his lip. 'Despite the hot chocolate I don't think I'm going to sleep just yet. Turn on the radio, there might be a repeat broadcast of a bullfight from Madrid.'

'A bullfight——'

'Of course,' he jibed, 'you British tend to hate them, don't you?'

'It's a cruel game.'

'*Conforme*, but life is cruel. Do as you are told, nurse, unless you want to upset your patient.'

'Heaven forbid!' Angie turned the dial of the radio until the unmistakable sounds of a *corrida* came on the air. Rique smoked and listened, his eyes blind slithers of steel, his lean cheeks stabbed by his dark sideburns, his skin so warmly brown in contrast to the bed linen.

'That bull is one son of a devil,' he murmured. 'You are still with me, Angel? You haven't dashed off in a huff?'

'I'm imagining those poor blindfolded horses,' she said.

'I know exactly how they feel,' he drawled.

Angie bit her lip; how too easy it was to forget he was blind because he looked so big and strong.

Lost in her thoughts, Angie came to with a start when Rique said to her: 'Don't break your heart, Angel, they've spared this brave bull.'

Her eyes were fixed upon him and her heart seemed

to have thunder in it. There on the radio music was playing amidst the roar of the crowd, *La Virgen de la Macarena*. Would *La Virgen* spare Rique, also a brave one who deserved to have his courage rewarded!

'You can switch off now,' said Rique. 'Brave of you to stay till the end.'

Words that might prove horribly significant, sending a shiver through Angie as she silenced the radio and the room went very quiet. 'I wish to God——' Rique broke off with a ragged sigh.

'I know, *amigo*.' She leaned over him and brushed his hair with her hand; his brow felt hot and anxiety quickened in her. 'Is your head aching?' she asked.

'Somewhere on the edges, but not too badly. I don't want to take one of those damned pills, they make me sleep like the dead and then—then I start to dream. You wouldn't like my dreams, Angel—I expect yours are about love and romance, eh?'

'Of course,' she said drily, 'we nurses have very torrid dreams.' She could guess the content of Rique's; she knew that the dreams of the blind were strangely more intense, more vivid than those of the sighted, and there was nothing to be done about it until Rique's memory of the bombing grew less focused and became, as it were, a blurred snapshot in his album of recollections.

'Have you a young man back in England?' he asked. 'Someone special with whom you walk hand in hand and make plans for the future? A young doctor, perhaps?'

'No one in particular, only the usual sort of dates.' She gazed into the unfathomable blindness of Rique's eyes while a pulse beat fast at the base of her throat.

Her hands wanted to touch his skin and her lips wanted to press against the cruel pucker of scars that, strangely enough, in no way spoiled his lean Latin looks. He wasn't handsome, not like his brother Seb; his attraction went deeper than that. He was rather like an *espada*, one of those who had been tossed by a bull in the arena and had looked into eyes of the shadow of the sword, whose name was Death.

'You must be tired as the damned,' he said abruptly. 'But before you go to your room do you think you could direct me to the bathroom?'

'Of course,' she said at once. 'Bathrooms are a hazard, aren't they? So many odd projections to hit yourself on.'

'One is also inclined, when brushing one's teeth, to spit in the wrong direction,' he drawled, pushing aside the bedcovers and sliding out so quickly that he came up against Angie before she could move away. He caught at her, his hand brushing inadvertently the bosom of her dress. *'Perdón!'* he said instantly. 'Not all projections are unpleasant, eh?'

She blushed as she took his hand and rested it upon her arm in the guiding position. How lean, tall and wickedly dark he was! How devastating he must have been in his uniform. She thought of those letters in his bedside drawer and wondered just how special the writer had been to him before he had decided that as a blind man he had become a burden.

'Rique,' she said, 'starting tomorrow you are going to Braille every part of the house which you'll be using, room by room, from the basement to the attics.'

'Angel, you have to be joking!'

'I happen to be quite serious.' She led him into the

bathroom, steering him away from shelves whose juttings could bruise him and startle him. 'Loo first, then teeth?'

'Please, nursie,' he said sardonically. 'In that order.'

'Here you are.' She placed his hand on the lid of the loo. 'The pedestal basin is to your right—can you manage?'

He grinned wickedly. 'I'd be perfectly happy to let you do the rest.' he drawled.

'I'm sure you would! I'll wait outside for you.'

When he came out of the bathroom there was a smear of toothpaste on his chin and as casually as possible she wiped it away with her handkerchief. 'I really do mean what I say about the house Brailling,' she said, as she led him back into his bedroom.

'Angel, I have lived here all my life——'

'Yes,' she agreed, 'but as a sighted person.'

She saw his lashes drop down over his eyes. 'You're blunt, and I remember you as a docile child—I believe I made you feel shy in those days.'

'We all grew up, Rique. You didn't imagine I stayed a child while you became a man?'

'It would seem not.' His nostrils drew in, tautening the blade-like lines of his nose.' "The shivering ghosts of many summers crowd." Does it strike you that way?'

'I like to think we were laughing ghosts, Rique. Always when I came to Bayaltar, when I went away again the sun seemed to die.'

'Was it our warm and lingering sun that brought you back again, Angel?'

'That among other things,' she agreed.

'Other things?'

'My—friends. I was always made so welcome, especially so after my—my dear aunt died.' Even to Rique, Angie chose to be loyal to the woman who had been her mother.

'You never had a large family, did you?' His lashes lifted and Angie was impaled by his blind eyes. 'Orphan Angel, eh?'

'If you like.'

'Who came to look upon us as your family, eh?'

'I like to think so. Your father is a most courteous and hospitable man, a true Spanish *grande*.'

'He is indeed.' One of Rique's hands had found a post of his bed and his fingers were tracing the carvings, decisively detailed like most Spanish craftsmanship. 'So at your insistence, nurse, I am to learn to toddle about my home at my ripe age.'

'You'll be fascinated by how unobservant you have been in the past, *amigo*, and I shall lead the way.'

'Are you going to put a collar and lead on me?'

'That won't be necessary. Touch will be your teacher and your fingertips will become your eyes. You have to gain confidence in your ability to get about your own home, and by Brailling the place for several days running you'll learn objects and they'll become your signposts to whichever room you wish to enter.'

'Will your room be on the agenda?' he drawled.

'I think it must be,' she said, in a voice she made efficient. 'There may be times when you need me and——'

'And?'

Her voice had wavered; it seemed impossible with Rique to be impersonal: things they said seemed to take on ulterior meaning and Angie was constantly aware of how he affected her.

'God,' he groaned, 'what sort of a life is it when a man has to grope about in the dark for what he wants? Angel, you are less than a shadow to me.'

'You say such charming things, *amigo*. I thought men of Latin blood were gallant towards women, even nurses.'

'Tell me, *mia niña*,' he asked, 'have you grown up pretty?'

'No.'

His lashes blinked. 'Well, that's the kind of modest statement I never expected to hear from a woman. I shall ask Seb to verify it the next time I see—'

Rique broke off, his face darkening. 'I shall never see my brother's face again,' he said harshly. 'God damn that bomb for not killing me outright! It was quick for the others, a white burning light, and then nothing more. God curse these eyes that can't see—there are moments when I could rip them out of my head!'

'Rique——' Angie ached to comfort him; it crossed her mind that she could lock his door and do so, but if his father ever found out, he would have her put out of the Residencia bag and baggage.

'Do you know what I'm thinking, Angel?'

'No, tell me.'

'That never again will I see a woman's creamy flesh.'

'You can touch it.'' She hesitated, then took his hand and laid it upon her bare arm, against the soft inner skin near the crook of her elbow.

'Mmm, your skin is cool and smooth.' He moved a finger back and forth along her arm.

He was standing so near and Angie realised that with his acute hearing he would catch the unsteady sound of her breathing. She drew away her arm and retreated from him. 'I'll tidy your bed and then you can get into it. You look worn out, Rique.'

'I'm sure I look repellent. Do I frighten you?'

'A hawk up close would also frighten me.' She smoothed his bedcovers and plumped his pillows, but still her heart seemed to beat uncomfortably fast. The lamplight, the bed, and Rique's tall figure were a confusing combination; if she had wondered if she loved him during the flight to the Spanish coast and the trip across water from the mainland, she was now convinced of it.

Never in her life had another person affected her so that her legs shook and she wanted to give herself regardless of what he felt for her.

'A hawk,' he said, 'has eyes that can spot a sparrow half a mile away.'

'Rique, you mustn't keep dwelling on it——'

'Easy for you to say! What do you know—a bit of a kid who came here because you think you owe my father some return for his generosity in the past.'

'That isn't true, Rique!' Her fingers clenched one of the bedposts as it to save herself from touching him; it would be like tinder to a spark but the flame that leapt wouldn't be a love flame. Rique was in no mood to love anyone; all he wanted right now was to hate everyone. Angie couldn't bear the thought of being hated by him, and being used to dull the edge of his pain.

'What is true?' he demanded. 'My father the Governor is a handsome man; have you some kind of crush on him?'

'Oh—what a thing to say!' She flinched as if he had

struck her around the face. 'There's no need to be
cruel to people just because—just think, Rique, of
what your friend Torcel de Byas has suffered.'

'True.' The anger drained from Rique's face and he
slumped down on the side of the bed; his hands
dragged themselves across the bones of his face. 'I will
get you to write to him; he's living in hell, so we'll
make good company for each other. Are my windows
open? I feel I'll suffocate if I can't breathe the sea air!'

Angie went to the windows and checked that they
were open. A misty moon hung in the sky over the sea
and the night air was still and scented by a thousand
mixed aromas, the sap in tall eucalyptus trees, stately
Spanish cedars and peppers, the silky-flowered mag-
nolias and the plumy jacarandas. She couldn't see
them clearly, but she knew they were there; the garden
of the Residencia had always been a beautiful, half-
wild place, up here on its plateau above the ocean.

An island, a house and a family which seemed to
say *Soy como soy*, I am as I am.

Angie took a deep breath of the air and thought of
the pool that was sheltered among the semi-tropical
trees, where waterlilies and the blue lotus spun softly
on the water, opening at daybreak and closing into
balls on the spread leaves when night fell.

For six years this house had figured in her dreams
and now it was real again, old, thick-walled, with an
air of Spanish secrecy and grace about it. She knew of
the private chapel attached by a shady cloister where
the *passifloras* grew and a great cloud of mauve bougainvillaea. There were Moorish archways with bold sculp-
turing around them, the fine mesh of wrought-iron
rejas, and tiling so perfectly laid it took the breath away.

It was a strange homecoming, with sorrow and joy intermingled. No longer did Rique walk into a room *avasallando*, his self-assurance fitting him as easily as a fine suit. Now his watchword was *cuidado* . . . and in a sense it was hers as well.

Beware . . . take care!

'Are you still there, *mia muchacha*?'

'I am here,' she turned to face him, 'until you don't need me any more.'

He absorbed her words as he slid into bed and lay back with his head pillowed upon his interlaced hands and spread arms. Angie could look right into his eyes and he didn't know; mica-grey eyes carved at a slight angle in his lean and swarthy face. He could have been a Moor, she thought, a Tarik who had lost the sight of both eyes.

'Would you,' he asked, 'give me the *coup de grâce* if I went mad?'

Her heart seemed to trip and her mouth went so dry she couldn't speak.

'Answer me, would you?'

'I—don't know,' she said faintly.

'I have shocked you, Angel?'

'It's defeatist talk, *amigo*. You have to think of getting well—of making yourself well.'

'To what purpose?' His eyes stared blindly across the room, fixing upon the wall between the windows where there was a painting in bold colours. Angie felt sure it was one of Seb's, painted in the days when he had been sure that he wanted to be an artist. Rique had never been unsure of what he wanted . . . and now he was asking if she would kill him if those metal fragments should destroy his reason. She shivered as cold drops of dread ran down her spine.

'Rique, you aren't yet destroyed as a man,' she said. 'You're a fighter, not a pacifist, so please——' Her voice choked to a halt; she couldn't go on as the tears smarted and fell hot down her cheeks. Furtively she brushed them away as if Rique could see them.

'What does a blind soldier do when he can't see to fire his gun?'

'He—he sets to and makes a constructive life for himself.'

'Doing what?'

'All sorts of things.'

'Such as?'

'You could train to be a lawyer.'

'That takes brains.'

'You have your share of those, Rique.'

'I had, Angel, but what I have inside my head right now is a time bomb and it could explode at any time— I have to face it, and so do you, and you have to promise me that you'll put my army pistol in my hand so I can finish myself——'

'I'll do no such thing!' she cried out.

'I demand it!' His expression was savage. 'There's no one else—you have to do it—you have to if I'm too crazed to know my own mind. *Dios mio*, that hospital where I was, there were men off their heads, raving half the time, and their own families afraid to see them like that. I can't face it—*I can't!*'

'Rique!' She was by his side so quickly her feet seemed not to touch the floor and driven by the need to console him, she had taken his head to her breast instinctively. 'My poor dear, you mustn't say and think such fearful things—I won't let you!'

He ground his face into her, gripping her until she felt her breath would stop in her throat. 'How can you stop me?' he groaned. 'I can't stop myself from thinking them. I have despair in my heart . . . I see nothing but blackness. It's all around me, inside me, and nothing can stop it but a bullet!'

'Don't—please!' She stroked his hair and felt the sweat that made it cling to his skull, yet he was shivering as if stone cold. She rocked him, murmured to him as if he were a child, until with the sudden savagery of a man he drew her down and found her mouth with bruising lips. Angie let him have his way and she knew with a cool head and a melting heart that she would stay with him if he wanted her and if it would ease the torment of his fears.

For endless moments their lips were locked, and then he was thrusting her away from him, so forcibly that she almost fell over, the heel of her left shoe buckling under her so she gave a gasp of pain.

'You see, I can only hurt people, and I wouldn't want the sacrifice of your virtue on my conscience. Go to your own bed, Angel. Suddenly I'm tired and I want to sleep,' his smile was a thin twist of the lips, 'perchance to dream.'

Angie didn't argue with him but tucked him in and turned out the bed lamp so his face was dimly lit by the moonglow through the windows.

'If you want anything in the night,' she said softly, 'I'm just next door, so don't hesitate to call me. Nurses sleep like cats, with one eye open. *Vaya con Dios,* Rique.' She left him quietly and closed the door so it was a few inches ajar. In her own room she sank down on the side of her bed and eased her shoes from her feet. She felt emotionally drained, but such was her training, and such was her caring that she knew she would sleep like a cat, alert for the slightest creak or groan from Rique's bedroom.

He was in a more desperate state than even his family realised, and with a little choked cry Angie rocked back and forth, stricken by a pain deep in her own vitals. This was love . . . love denied the romance of silvery starlight, music drifting across water, and cherishing kisses. This was love for a man who cried out against his blinded starlight.

Waves of despair swept over Angie, then at last she straightened her spine and set her jaw. Starting tomorrow she would take his hand and lead him out into the sunlight and make him feel it on his skin; she would take him into the water and into town and make him listen to the pulse of life again.

She wouldn't allow her mind to dwell on the dread possibility that one day his plea for a bullet in his brain would have to be faced. She and Rique together would live each hour as if it were a day, and with that resolve lifting her heart a little she went to the niche in the wall near her bed and touched the blue cloak of the beautiful Madonna who occupied the niche.

Would *La Virgen* be merciful and spare Rique de Zaldo?

CHAPTER FIVE

ANGIE's days began early because it was customary for her to rise with the sun. She would shower, put on her deep-blue uniform, pin on her cap, slide her feet into her low-heeled shoes, and then go quietly into Rique's room to see if he was still sleeping.

Some mornings he lay there very still among his tangled coverings, a sign that he had slept restlessly before going in to a deep slumber. Sometimes he lay there awake, smoking one of his dark *cigarillos*. The fact that he had taught himself to be so adept at lighting the *cigarillo* was an indication he seemed unaware of, that his touch perception was very good.

It certainly gave Angie a line of hope to cling to, but for the time being she put only light pressure on him, insisting that each day he do his Brailling of the house he had been born in. His blindness meant that he had to learn to use his other senses until they were so finely tuned that he would never find himself lost in the house and would be able to navigate its stairs and corridors with confidence, judging by touch, smell and instinct exactly where he was.

It pleased her that he had become interested in the game, as he called it, and already he had mastered the ground-floor rooms. The family and staff had grown used to seeing the pair of them patrolling the house, with Rique walking a hand-touch behind her, using his own hands to memorise projections, objects, carv-

ings and corners until he could finally fool a stranger
that he could actually see where he was going.

Now and again there were setbacks for Angie to
contend with; still he was liable to fall into black, de-
spairing silences, and then he would start drinking and
would be bitterly sarcastic if she told him he was
doing himself more harm than good.

'Take yourself to hell, Angel, and don't bore me
with your pious preaching,' he would say, not shout-
ing but saying the words in a voice of brutal insolence
far more hurtful than anger would have been. She
tried to keep bottles of drink out of his reach, but
somehow he always managed to get hold of one and
she suspected that Ysabel supplied him with the Spanish brandy he liked; his fire-water, as he called it.

Angie thought of going to Don Carlos with her suspicion, but she wasn't by nature a sneak, nor did she
want Rique's father to think she couldn't cope with
the situation. She could only hope that Rique would
ease off the brandy as he began to realise that he was
making headway and learning how to combat the terrors and frustrations of his dark world.

This particular morning Angie switched on her
radio, keeping the music soft as she prepared for the
day ahead of her. Doris Day was singing in her inimit-
able style *I'll never stop loving you* . . . and the song
induced in Angie a sense of poignancy. *My love for
you will live till time itself is through.*

Comb in hand, she stood at her window and saw a
sky as smooth as blue silk, and a sea that was littered
with immense globules of sunlight, gold shot with
silver, trapped in the water.

The song throbbed into stillness and a sigh escaped

her. Sometimes the lyric and melody of a popular song could be as moving and evocative as a profound piece of classical music, or even the love duet from *La Bohème*. Life, she reflected, wasn't so far removed from melodrama at times. Here she was, resident nurse in the rambling island home of an *hidalgo*, loving and caring for a blinded soldier who might not survive his injuries.

When she had spoken with Dr Romaldo and received her instructions regarding Rique she had asked what his chances were; the Spanish doctor had spread his hands. 'Who knows?' he had said. 'I felt it was best not to build up too high the hopes of Don Carlos. His son still carries splinters of metal deep inside his head, so embedded that the risk of their removal was not to be contemplated. The surgeon may have given him six months to live a fairly normal life, but nature in her unexpected way may extend that into years. *Dios sabe!* Rique has *fuerza*, he gets it from his father, but what he needs above all is the will to face a world he can no longer see.'

That sea out there, Angie thought, as beautiful as a Turner painting. Rique could smell it, and he could hear the cries of the seabirds as they fished for their breakfast, but never could he feast his eyes on the sheer wonder of the Bayaltar sun spilling across the aeons of water. Only memories of it were stored in his mind . . . just as she was trapped there as a schoolgirl of sixteen with plaits loosening from their ties and socks of sand halfway up her legs.

Slim, trim and feeling crisply efficient in her uniform, Angie went into Rique and found him out on his balcony, leaning there with his blind eyes fixed on the shimmering sea, a *cigarillo* clenched between his lips, a corded silk dressing-gown open against the bare, bronze-hard chest against which the sun was striking.

'*Buenos días*, Rique. You had good repose, *amigo*?'

'Not too bad. It smells and feels like a wonderful morning.' Smoke drifted over his shoulder, past the wrought-iron of the balcony that was a mass of tangled tiny white bells giving off the scent that later on the heat of the sun would obscure.

'Torcal de Byas arrives today,' she reminded him. 'We've promised to meet him at the dock.'

'I hadn't forgotten.' A brief smile caught at his lip. 'Why is it you always sound bossy when you are wearing your uniform?'

'Uniforms do that to people. I'm sure you kept your men on their toes when you were wearing yours.'

'True,' he murmured. 'We'll have breakfast out here, shall we?'

'We certainly shall.' Rique still wasn't keen on eating his meals with the family, though he had consented once or twice to dine with them in the evening. Angie always took breakfast with him, then the valet would arrive to shave and help him dress. Actually he was getting so adept at both, though the use of an electric razor meant that he had to shave twice a day, that he could have dispensed with the manservant. But it had been his father's idea that he have a personal servant and so Rique complied.

There was a firm bond between Don Carlos and his eldest son, yet Angie had noticed that Rique was always rather formal with him . . . only with her did he seem to voice the fears that sometimes awoke him at night, sweating from every pore, with his heart hammering his ribs.

'Don't tell anyone,' he would beg of her. 'I don't want Padre worried more than he is; he has his work and enough responsibilities to cope with. Let it be our secret that I have these nightmares.'

'What do you fancy this morning?' Angie enquired.

He considered, his eyes staring straight into the sun. 'Coffee, half of grapefruit, grilled ham and tomatoes, and maybe a couple of almond buns.'

Angie's eyes widened with a quick delight. 'You are hungry this morning, *amigo*.'

'So I am,' he drawled. 'That's all the exercise you keep insisting on; you must by now be acquainted with every stick and stone of this house, the times you have made me Braille it.'

'It's a fine old house,' she smiled. 'A real mixture of Moorish Spain, as you are.'

'As I am?' He quirked an eyebrow. 'My mother was as fair as you.'

'I know that, but like your father you have a certain look——'

'You mean I look like an Arab?'

'Yes, your skin and eyes——' She broke off, confusedly. 'I'll go and ring down for breakfast——'

'Angel.'

'Yes?'

'Do my eyes look blind?'

'No.'

'It isn't that I'm conceited, but when we go into town today I don't want people to stare at me.'

'Women will stare at you, Rique, but not because you're blind.' She quickly entered his bedroom and went to the house phone, where she rang down for his breakfast, requesting orange juice and waffles for herself. When she turned from the phone Rique was standing between the windows of the balcony and her heart gave a little jump. She seemed never to get used to how much she loved the look of him; the more she was with him the harder it grew to be impersonal.

'When a woman compliments a Spaniard, she's tempting the devil,' he drawled. 'Or was that a little bit of therapy?'

'A bit of each,' she said lightly. 'You're a big chip off your father, so you must know what you look like——'

'You very much like the Don my father, don't you, Angel?'

'I like Don Carlos enormously,' she admitted. 'He typifies all that the British admire in the Spanish character. He has a splendid appearance, a warm heart, and the kind of courtesy that women associate with gentlemen.'

'You have a soft spot for gentlemen, eh?'

'Most women do,' she said without hesitation. 'Without them the world will turn into a terrible place. Honour and integrity will vanish, and good manners with them.'

'I thought women these days were ready to relinquish the held-open door, the kiss on the hand, and the ring before the wedding night?'

'It's a fairytale,' she said with conviction. 'I've worked with nurses who have had affairs and then regretted them when they've actually fallen in love. They hate feeling shopworn and they worry in case it gets to their boy-friends that they've played around.'

'Something you've never done, eh?'

'Something I've never wanted to do—at least, not just as a fling.'

'You are saving yourself for your true love, a sentiment my father would approve of with every bone in
his Spanish body.'

'Isn't it a sentiment you approve of, Rique?' Her
eyes moved over his face with its traces of old conti-
nents and its mingling of pride and passion. 'I'm not
going to believe that you would marry a woman who
had belonged to some other man.'

'There might have been a time——' He shrugged
and went out on the balcony again, his words flung
back over his shoulder. 'Now I shall never marry. No
woman was meant to have the kind of strength and
patience that a blind man would command. A woman
needs to be the protected, not the protector.'

'She might love you enough not to mind about that,'
Angie said, following him outside, her heart coming
into her throat when she saw that he had gone very
close to the edge of the balcony, with its long drop to
the stony court below. As casually as possible she went
to him, took him by the arm and led him to the cane-
work table and chairs.

'What a husband I'd make!' he jibed, as he sat
down. 'No, it's up to my brother Seb to carry on the
Zaldo name, and you, Angel, might be the perfect
partner to assist him in doing so. Shall I,' he added
wickedly, 'ask my father to arrange a marriage between you?'

'You dare!' She managed not to sound as hurt as she
felt that he should so casually link her with his
brother. He couldn't see and couldn't seem to sense
that it was *he* who dominated her feelings. The care
she gave him he took for granted as the regulation care
of a nurse for her patient.

'I might very well dare, then you will be part of a

family and you will be my sister. Wouldn't you like that?'

No, her heart cried. Oh no!

'You don't seem very enthusiastic about the idea, *mia amada*.'

'I'm not.'

'Is it me as a brother you don't fancy, or Seb as a husband?'

'I don't fancy having my life arranged, thank you.'

'Leaving it up to *el destino*?'

'It's the best way, don't you think?'

'I'm Spanish with a dash of the Moor,' he mocked. 'I don't happen to think that young women always know what's best for them—my brother is a splendid fellow and you could do a hell of a lot worse than to love him.'

'He may not want to love me,' she said in exasperation. 'Look, I think we should change the topic of conversation before it becomes an argument.'

'You look, Angel, do you think I don't know that Seb took you out that time he was in England on business? He told Maya and my sister told me, the big brother she has a habit of confiding in. She seemed desperately keen on the idea of you and Seb becoming a team, and I must confess that I rather like the idea myself, and I'm sure my father the Don would approve of having you in the family.'

Angie gazed at Rique with a look of pain in her eyes. 'Yes,' she said, 'I did go out on a couple of dates with Seb and he's still the charming person he was in the old days, but I shall hate you, Rique, and never forgive you if you put the idea in his head that I—I want to marry him. It isn't, you know, any of your business!'

'Ah, has the blind man put his foot in it?'

'Now you're playing for my sympathy,' she reproved.

'I'm not a very nice person, am I, Angel?'

'Not at the moment,' she agreed.

'Not half as nice as Seb, nor anywhere as courteous as my father. If you came back to Bayaltar on their behalf, then you're paying a high price in having me on your hands.'

'Perhaps,' she dared to say, 'I came back on your behalf.'

'Are you a glutton for punishment?' he drawled. 'That's all I have to offer, unlike Seb who has all his faculties and is going places in the world . . . the world of bright lights and glamour, of limousines and premieres. Don't you find the thought exciting?'

'It thrills me to bits,' she said sarcastically. 'Please stop trying to arrange a marriage for me. I'm not a Spanish girl; I'm a nurse with a career to think about—and now let's drop the subject and have breakfast.'

Maria the maid carried the tray out to the balcony table; in a little glass flute there was a brilliant red rose, half out of its bud.

'How lovely!' Angie exclaimed.

'Don Carlos cut it for you, *señorita*. He said it reminds him of a song he likes, *Rose of England*.'

'Oh yes, I know it.' Angie flushed and was very aware of Rique's attention. 'Please thank His Excellency for me, Maria.'

'*Si, señorita.*' The girl's big brown eyes dwelt on Rique with a kind of awe mixed with pity; he looked so big and vital sitting there, and his eyes seemed too alive to be sightless. As if aware he was being stared at, his hand clenched the edge of the table and Angie said quickly:

'*Gracias*, Maria, everything looks very tasty.'

The girl smiled and withdrew, and Angie poured coffee. 'Rose of England?' Rique murmured.

'It's a beauty,' she said in a matter-of-fact voice. 'Red as flame. I'll wear it on my lapel when we go into town. There you are, *amigo*, coffee at three-fifteen, food at three-thirty and bread roll at three-forty-five.'

This clock-like arrangement of his food made it possible for him to eat without fumbling about for what he wanted. He found his coffee with ease and sprinkled sugar between his spread fingers on to his pink-fleshed grapefruit.

'Mmm, very nice,' he commented as he spooned the fruit. 'Are you having the same?'

'No, orange juice and waffles—delicious!'

'Has anyone ever told you, Angel, that you have a rather delicious voice with a curious little break in it?'

She gave him a startled look, a piece of waffle poised on her fork.

'Silence speaks louder than words,' he said sardonically. 'I suppose when we can see people's faces we don't always notice voice inflections. I am learning, am I not?'

'Your perceptions are very good indeed.' That single compliment and all the sting had gone out of his taunts that she should get together with his brother. Love . . . it was so disarming that it was like being on an emotional seesaw. The ups were madly exhilarating, but the downs made you feel as if you'd been dropped on your heart. Anyway, that was how it was for her, with no happy medium. Being with Rique was all sun, or all shadow.

Quickly and quietly she replaced his finished grape-fruit with his plate of grilled ham and tomatoes and placed the butter dish within reach of his hand. He was rarely clumsy when he ate alone with her and she watched in a kind of fascination as he broke his bread roll in his lean hands and applied butter with neat swipes of the knife. Then with the guidance of a finger he found his ham and cut it himself and carried the piece straight to his mouth.

To the sighted each of these actions was child's play, but for Rique they were small victories. They were teaching him that he could be his own master again; that one day he would be able to walk out of this house with only his cane to guide his steps. A seeing-eye dog was being trained for him at a kennels in England, but it would be a few weeks yet before the Labrador bitch could be brought to Bayaltar. Don Carlos didn't trust the purchase of a dog from Spain because, as he said, there was always the danger of rabies and he didn't want further suffering to visit his son.

Angie touched a fingertip to the red rose. Her own father would always be unknown, and she envied Maya for having a father like the Don of Bayaltar even if he had forbidden her to associate with a divorced man. Maya had always been very protected and Angie suspected that it had been the glamour of the singing guitarist which had attracted her. He had gone off to entertain at a hotel on the Costa del Sol and the very fact that Maya had not gone with him seemed to indicate that she preferred to remain under her father's roof.

Angie didn't blame her; it was a very handsome roof, for the Residencia had a rather splendid dominance about it ... a mixture of Iberian and Moorish architecture which had survived into a more modern age and yet retained its look of guarded women, of intrigue, power and a dash of romance. Angie admired it inside and out; the subdued richness of its rooms, dark and silky woodwork, a lacelike tracery of iron, and archways shaped like half-moons leading to tree-shaded patios.

Far away in England the house had sometimes seemed like a half-forgotten dream ... it had seemed impossible that anything could be so perfect, but each day here she rediscovered parts of the dream. When Rique wanted to smoke alone in the garden room, she would wander about on her own and had ventured up into the *atalaya*, startling the guard who had been taking his siesta instead of keeping watch. It didn't seem possible on sunlit Bayaltar that any sort of harm could come to the Governor's family, but Rique was the living proof of the troubles going on in the Basque country, stirred up by fanatics who used violence indiscriminately in order to have their way.

Sometimes he talked about it and Angie didn't try to stop him. The violence which had blinded him had to find its way out of his system; those slithers of steel-hot memory were as destructive as the actual slithers of steel in his head and when he wanted to talk about that day and the other members of the patrol who had died, then Angie listened and was thankful that he was unable to see how his words affected her. Graphic words about blood and pain and the young soldier who had shrieked his wife's name as he died of his appalling wounds.

The young wife, Rique said, who was due to have a baby.

'I could go another cup of coffee.' His request broke in on her thoughts. 'You are still with me?'

'I was thinking.' She poured coffee for both of them and added cream to her own; Rique liked his black and strong as army coffee.

'About Torcal de Byas? I imagine a woman would be curious, but don't expect someone monklike. He's a man of the world with a dash of Scots blood—hence his name; he was prowling about getting material for his syndicated news column when he got hurt; the nearest hospital treating his kind of injury was a military one and that is how we came to meet. God pity the kind of adjustment he has to make!'

'Is he a married man?' Angie asked.

'A widower. I believe that is how he came to be in an area where fighting was going on; he only spoke once about his wife and I could tell that he still hadn't got over her death. He had taken her on one of his news-hunting trips, their first together, and she was knocked down by a motorcyclist as she crossed a road to buy some cakes. She lay in a coma for seven weeks; he said they tried everything. He'd talk at her bedside by the hour, they played music she had been fond of, but she just went deeper into the coma until she finally stopped breathing. Torcal said he was still talking to her when they told him she had stopped living. They had been married just three months.'

'Poor man!' Angie felt a thrill of coldness go through her. 'He's certainly had his share of trouble.'

'Yes,' Rique frowned. 'I've been brought up to believe in the ethics of Christ, but it would sometimes seem that goodness demands a forfeit . . . often a crucifixion. I have discussed this with Padre and we ended up in an argument. He's Spanish to the backbone.'

'Aren't you, Rique?'

'In certain ways, perhaps. You are a nurse, Angel. You must have noticed that suffering seems to afflict the good more often than it attacks the bad. Haven't you asked yourself why?'

'Yes,' she said quietly. 'Perhaps it's a kind of test. My own—aunt, she was kind and good, but her life was a hard-working, anxious one, and she wore herself out. Perhaps selfishness is an armour that unselfish people lack? Anyway, I wouldn't want to be selfish, would you?'

His fingers sought for an almond bun, but instead of eating it Rique crumpled it into pieces. 'I sit in the garden room and think of many things,' he replied. 'Blindness creates a mental screen upon which the images and memories play one upon another and I wonder what it is that leads people on to the paths which they take, sometimes to a dead end. It is in human nature to be able to plan and look ahead; to anticipate the future and the pleasures it might hold.'

He sighed and his blind eyes searched the darkness in which Angie knew she had no face or form; she was a voice he sometimes listened to, a hand he occasionally held. Across the table he was looking not at her, but he thought he was, his gaze beyond her across the balcony iron to where the sea shimmered into the far horizon.

'If I had chosen to enter my uncle's law firm,' he said reflectively, 'then would I still be facing a blank wall, with no door I can open into a garden where I see the bright flowers and where someone waits to greet me?'

'Rique,' she said, 'you can touch and smell the flowers—hold out your hand.'

He did so and she placed upon his palm the red rose which his father had sent to her, its petals soft and cool, its stem damp from the water in the flute.

'Your rose, eh?' He carried it to his nostrils and breathed its scent. 'As you say, I can feel it and I can smell it, but for me it's still a black rose.'

Words that stayed with Angie while she dressed to drive Rique into town to meet the newspaper man he had become friendly with in hospital. Two men whom fate had deprived of the ability to lead the confident, active life that so many people enjoyed without giving it a thought that it was marvellous to have unimpaired senses and the ability to love and raise a family.

For Rique the roses might always be black, and for Torcal de Byas there could never again be a full sexual relationship with a woman. Angie cinched the belt of her dress and wondered, along with Rique, why the path of duty led so often to adversity. It seemed so horribly unfair when the selfish and insensitive seemed never to experience undue pain or setback.

She combed her hair into sleekness and selected a bag and gloves to match her dress which was of cream bouclé with delicate *pointelle* work on the bodice and sleeves. After inspecting herself in the mirror Angie decided that she looked cool and personable, and went next door to see if Rique was ready; his manservant was tidying up and told her the *señor* had gone downstairs and was waiting for her there.

Angie found him in the *sala* and she allowed herself the luxury of looking at him from top to toe. He wore close white trousers and a tan shirt only a shade darker than his skin, a brimmed Cordoban hat concealed his scars and his overall look was one of dark striking suppleness. When he stood still it was always hard to accept that he was blind.

'*Señor*, you are quite splendid,' Angie informed him.

'And what are you wearing, *mia amada*, not your uniform, I hope?' Using his cane and nostrils tensed to draw in the scent of the Blue Grass she was wearing, he came directly to where she stood, unmoving except for the racing of her heart as he ran a hand down the fabric of her dress, just clingy enough to cause him to touch the shape of her with his fingers.

'Feels nice—what colour is the dress?'

'Cream.' Her breathing was irregular and she felt a molten longing to be crushed close to his tallness; her eyes were filled with his lean face, so Spanish beneath the brim of the Cordoban hat.

'Are you wearing your rose?' His fingers moved and found it pinned to her lapel, attached with the golden horseshoe which had belonged to the mother she had always called Aunt Kit. It had been among her few belongings, along with the documents which had revealed the secret of Angie's birth.

Rique's fingers touched her hair, then swiftly they were removed as he swung away from her, his quick ears catching the sound of a footfall before she did. It wasn't only his hearing that was acute, but several times just recently she had seen him pull up short even as he seemed about to walk into an object. She knew that the facility was called facial vision, a kind of extra-sensory perception by which the sightless sensed danger as a vibration against the skin of the face. It excited her, but she hadn't yet discussed it with him; she wanted to choose the right moment, when he was relaxed enough to accept that facial vision was a gift which not every blinded person was granted.

'Rique *mio*,' his sister Maya had entered the room, 'you are all dressed up! Where is Angie taking you?'

'We're going into town to meet a friend of mine who is coming to stay on the island for a while. Are you doing anything yourself, Maya?'

'No.' She plunged her hands into the pockets of a pair of rather scruffy jeans. 'There's nothing much to do—everything's such a bore; not like the old days when we used to go sailing and exploring. I feel sometimes as if every bit of fun is over!'

'Don't talk bilge,' her brother said cuttingly. 'You're young and healthy, and you bore everyone else the way you are sulking over your first bit of heartache. If that guitarist had felt all that deeply about you, then he'd have carried you off with him and you would have let him, disregarding Padre's lack of approval. My suggestion, my girl, is that you go and put on a fetching dress and come with Angel and myself to meet this friend of mine.'

Maya stood and considered the invitation. 'Are you lunching with him in town?' she asked.

Rique didn't answer, so Angie took the bull by the horns. 'I think that would be very enjoyable,' she said. 'Shall we do that, Rique?'

He gripped the handle of his cane and seemed as if he would strike out at her for suggesting he eat in a public place. 'I think not——'

'Now who's being a bore?' It was Maya who spoke. 'Rique *mio*, who cares a fig if you drop a potato off your fork or put pepper on your pudding? You are *you* and there isn't another man on this island who can hold a candle to you! Do let us go and lunch at the Casa de las Palmas where we used to go for a treat in the old days! Do say yes!'

For moments on end the room seemed thunderous, as if all their heartbeats were pounding together for different emotional reasons. 'Very well,' the words came suddenly from Rique. 'If it will stop you from brooding over that young man, Maya, then we will go and lunch at the Casa.'

Angie breathed a sigh of relief, while Maya promptly threw her arms around her brother's neck. 'You darling!'

'That's as maybe.' He fingered his sister's hair. 'This feels like a bird's nest—go and give it a good brushing, then put on something that will cheer up a man who has had a rough time of it. Be brisk! Angel and I will wait in the car for you.'

'Why do you always call her that?' Maya gazed at him inquisitively, as if he could see her.

'That's what nurses are, are they not?' He pushed her away from him. 'Mine in particular has to be rather angelic in order to put up with me.'

Maya smiled at Angie. 'Is he very terrible at times?'

'A devil, but he's improving. One of these evenings I'm going to take him to the top of the *atalaya* so I can describe the sunset to him—they were always very Turner-like, weren't they?'

'And so romantic,' Maya murmured. 'The steps up to the watchtower are narrow and winding—do you think he has the breath for it at his age?'

'Go and get dressed,' he ordered. 'Men of my age are in their prime.'

'Are they, Angie?' Maya ran from the *sala* laughing

to herself, while Rique fingered the raised dial of his watch whose crocodile strap meshed with the dark hairs of his wrist, dark and very male against the cuff of his shirt.

'That young man hurt her pride, I think,' he said. 'Padre is a shrewd judge of character and I believe he would have accepted him for Maya despite the divorce had he thought him genuinely in love with her. In some ways Maya is a shy girl and we are an affluent family; he was probably on the make. Perhaps next time she will be luckier in love.'

'Let's hope so,' said Angie, with a slightly wistful smile. With Rique's arm tucked through hers they went out to the car, a Mercedes which belonged to his father.

When they had settled themselves inside she said to him: 'You're very Latin in your own attitudes towards women, aren't you? I believe you sometimes resent me because you have to accept my help.'

'It's natural.' From the passenger seat at her side he reached out and slapped the wheel in front of her. 'How do you think I feel, having to rely on a woman to drive me and lead me about?'

'I know it isn't easy to accept, but you're making headway.' She pondered a moment, then took the plunge. 'You must have realised by now that you have facial sensitivity and it's very important to you, a kind of seventh sense.'

'*Dios mio*, am I supposed to be in seventh heaven because of it?' Rique looked sardonic as he leaned back in his seat. 'I want to see things, not merely feel them—like damned spiders brushing my face.'

'Is that how it feels, Rique?'

'Something like that.'

'You ought to be thrilled,' she urged. 'It's something special that when you walk too close to objects you feel a kind of vibration from them.'

'There are certain objects that give me a thrill,' he drawled. 'They aren't closed doors, nor brick walls. They are soft and warm and curved—but I mustn't have naughty thoughts, must I? They aren't good for the patient.'

'Rique, I don't interfere with your thoughts—whatever they are.'

'Don't you?' he growled. 'There are times when I wish you would go and nurse some genteel old lady.'

'Rique, what's the matter?' Angie gave him a rather bewildered look. 'Why are you trying to pick a quarrel with me? What have I said or done?'

He sat silent a moment, then released a pent-up breath. 'It's the way you are always so damn optimistic. What sort of a life do you think this is for a man—I curse the day I got born *for this*! But you—you prattle on about facial sensitivity as if I had my sight back! Do I make myself plain, nurse, if my real vision is never going to return, then to hell with living! I don't want years of this half-life!'

'Rique——' She spoke his name in a stricken way.

'I will strangle you with my bare hands, Angel, if you tell me once again that I can feel the sun's warmth even if I can't see it up there in the blue sky. It's like telling me I can feel a kiss—yes, but what I want is to see the look that welcomes my mouth on a woman's! Do I make myself clear?'

'Perfectly clear when you use your barrack room voice, and it's clear enough that you're feeling sorry for yourself, and all because you've let Maya talk you into lunching at a restaurant. The people there will be too busy eating their own lunch to watch avidly as you eat yours!'

'So I've rattled the Girl Guide, have I?' As he spoke his hand sought her knee and she tensed as his hard fingers closed upon her leg and began deliberately to stroke it. 'Warm and smooth and curved, Angel. You must have a few sensuous feelings to match?'

'M-my feelings are my own business.' Bracing herself, she slapped his hand off her leg; she didn't want him touching her in that insolent way. 'I don't like weak and cowardly talk about life not being worthwhile—your friend Torcal has more to grouse about than you! You can marry and have children——'

'A wife and *niños* I shall never see?' He gave a curt laugh. 'One of these days Dr Romaldo is going to find the nerve to tell me what I know already, that the metal I'm still carrying in my brain is going to blow my reason to shreds. Marry, Angel, with that prospect hanging over me? You must be out of your tiny mind!'

'Don't, Rique—please!' Angie laid a hand to his lips. 'You hurt yourself and you—you hurt me when you talk in that way.'

'You mean I disappoint you, *bebe*. You thought you were turning me into an obedient patient, eh?'

'You seemed to be responding.' She trailed a finger to his scarred temple. 'Don't give in, Rique. There's still a hell of a lot of fight in you and you're facing the biggest battle of your life. Don't you want to be a winner?'

'The odds are stacked,' he said broodingly. 'The enemy is inside my head and I can't fight an enemy I can't see.'

'Don't be bitter,' she pleaded.

'Wouldn't you be full of gall if you stood in my shoes?'

'Perhaps——'

'There is no perhaps about it, *niña*. The roses are black in the garden where I walk, and the women have no faces.'

'Rique——' He couldn't see the pain that twisted her face. 'Are you trying to make me cry?'

'No,' he shook his head, 'I'm trying to make you understand once and for all.'

'I do understand, believe me!'

'Then tell me what I'm going to do with my life, always supposing I have one ahead of me?'

'I told you, you could train to be a lawyer. You have a sharp mind.'

'For how long, eh? Even as we sit here discussing my future, those pieces of steel could shift and send me crazy.'

'Even if that's true,' she forced herself to say, 'you can't spend your days sitting in a chair, waiting for it to happen. You were a soldier and trained to take chances—you always knew there might be a bullet with your name on it—or a bomb waiting to explode in your face.'

'So easy for you to say, Angel, but the suspense is killing me by inches. When I sleep I dream, and you know what I dream! When I lie there awake I find myself straining to see the starlight through the windows—you can't know the emptiness and loneliness of it, a great black shadow that just won't shift. I—I never knew what fear was until this cursed fate fell on me!'

'My dear——' Suddenly she couldn't bear the

things he was saying and was driven to press her lips to his in order to stop the words.

'Don't do that——' He thrust her away from him. 'Don't pity me!'

'You're too strong to be pitied—I just want to share your pain.'

'You don't know what you're saying.' He spoke savagely. 'Just as I can't share your blue sky, you can't share my black one. Don't get sentimental, nurse, I'd sooner have you optimistic.'

He sank back in his seat and turned his face away from her. Angie gazed at the lean distinction of his profile and saw the jerk of the muscle beside his mouth. Her heart and bones ached inside her; a silence lapsed and lengthened, broken as Maya came to the car and climbed into the back of it. She had groomed her hair and was wearing a dress with cap sleeves, brightly splashed with colours. Her lips were poppy-red to match one of the colours.

'Have you smartened yourself up?' Rique demanded.

'Is your friend such a charmer?' she asked.

Angie felt her nerves tighten up at the question; what Rique had confided to her about Torcal de Byas was too private and stark to be passed on to Maya. Because her life had been more protected than Angie's, such a revelation might be shocking to her, making it difficult for her to behave naturally with him when she met him.

With Angie behind the wheel the Mercedes coasted smoothly down the gradient that led on to the road to the centre of Bayaltar; there was an opalescent mist afloat on the sea, which was pearl-blue and very still.

'What is the sea looking like?' Rique enquired, having ignored his sister's query about Torcal.

'As if your favourite painter had put it on canvas,' she replied. 'Do you still consider Turner the greatest of all landscape artists?'

'I don't alter my opinions once I've formed them,' he said.

'What an arrogant devil you can be, Rique!' Maya leaned forward from her seat and stroked the nape of his neck, pushing her fingers beneath the hard brim of his Cordoban hat. 'Is your friend anything like you?'

'Not really. What we have in common are our scars.'

'I rather like your scars,' she said, winding her arms about him. 'You feel strong and tough, big brother, the one who always took charge of us in the old days. How long and golden were those days, and how we laughed and played and it never seemed to rain. Do you remember, *querido*?'

'Most of it,' he drawled. 'There were blanks, especially when I first came home from hospital, but now I recollect things with more clarity. I can't seem to remember if Angel was pretty or plain.'

'Does it matter?' Angie smiled slightly as she drove along a bypass foaming with mauve bougainvillaea, leading towards the Chapel of the Lilies, with its creaky turntable at the entrance, and an iron bell in its narrow tower. Some venerable old trees shaded the chapel and the lovely old windows aglow with painted lilies. It was there in the chapel cemetery that Rosa de Zaldo was at rest in the family vault, and Angie was glad when they had left the place behind them.

'How do you imagine Angie?' Maya asked her brother.

'She is trapped in the amber of some far-off day, Maya *mia*, when she had plaits and bashful eyes.'

'Do you like that description of yourself, Angie?' Maya was laughing a little, but the look she gave Angie was a questioning one, as if it had suddenly dawned on her that they were adults now and subject to feelings and longings they no longer confided with the eagerness of schoolgirls.

'We all have something we have to live with,' said Angie, with more lightness than she felt. She drove the car into the parking area alongside the dock where the launches unloaded the passengers they brought across from Spain. She slid from the driving seat and walked round to assist Rique; his lips were slightly quirked as he gripped her elbow.

'Yes, I remember you as a child,' he murmured, 'but when I touch you, Angel, you turn into somebody I don't quite know.'

'What are you two whispering about?' Maya wanted to know, and the look she had given Angie was transferred to her brother.

'I was merely asking my nurse if my hat is on at the correct angle,' he said sardonically. 'One of the peculiar things about being blind is that clothing loses its social significance. If I had been brought into town in my nightshirt I wouldn't be any the wiser.'

'Oh—Rique!' If he had meant to amuse Maya his remark had the opposite effect upon her. Her lips quivered and her brown eyes filled with tears. 'I—I can hardly bear it when you t-talk like that.'

'I thought I was being witty,' he drawled. 'Dry your eyes, *niña*—ah yes, I know you have gone all weepy. Angel will inform you that I have the hearing of a cat, and that objects bounce a warning vibration on to my skin . . . a sort of seventh sense, as she calls it.'

'Truly?' Maya stood there looking very young as a teardrop rolled down her cheek and slid to the corner of her mouth. 'Rique, does that mean——?'

'It probably does, little one.' His tone of voice was almost casual. 'I expect it's nature's way of compensating for my eyes. Now, shall we go and meet Torcal?'

CHAPTER SIX

THE sun was hot and the sea was glittering as fishermen hauled net loads of fish into the harbour, calling to each other, singing and arguing. Ramshackle houses were built along the rambling harbour walls, made picturesque by dazzling vines that clothed the sun-cracked façades. Cobbled alleys and steep, twisting lanes wended their way from the harbour, with balconies jutting overhead and providing shade from the sun, plants trailing through the curlicued iron.

It was an island old in history where the rich, dark sound of Catholic church bells was heard alongside the call to prayer from the mosque towers. Women clothed all in black, their faces veiled to the eyes, shopped in the bazaars, while dark-eyed Spanish girls served in the medley of shops along the Ramblas de las Virtudes.

Because the island was situated in the Mediterranean its invasions had been varied and this showed in the looks of the people and in the architecture of their dwellings. It didn't take a lot of imagination to envisage Moorish pirates plundering the shops and leaping the walls of the Spanish houses to drag the young girls from their loudly protesting *dueñas*.

Angie was very aware of the atmosphere as she stood with Maya and Rique as the midday launch came cutting through the satin-blue sea towards the dock.

'What's he like?' Maya twined an arm through Rique's.

'How would I know, *niña*? We met in the hospital and I wasn't likely to ask the nurses if he was handsome.'

'Why not? It seems a perfectly reasonable thing to ask.'

'My dear innocent,' Rique laughed briefly, 'no wonder you fell for a plausible entertainer! I'm not gay, and neither is Torcal!'

'Oh——' Maya blushed. 'I see.'

'The launch is coming in now,' Angie told Rique. The passengers soon began to alight and Angie watched them and wondered herself what kind of a man Torcal de Byas was. He had suffered so much and it might well have made him harsh and bitter.

The jetty gradually cleared, and then she noticed a man loitering in the shadow of a doorway; she could see that he held a suitcase and she had a feeling he was Torcal de Byas who for some reason hesitated to approach and introduce himself. Was it because he had spotted Maya, who looked so young and girlish in her bright, cap-sleeved dress? Had he become withdrawn from the company of women? In the circumstances it would be understandable.

'What the devil——' Rique fingered the dial of his watch. 'Hasn't he arrived on the noon launch?'

'I rather think I can see him,' Angie murmured.

'Rique, perhaps he wasn't expecting you to be with—with Maya and myself.'

'Torcal knows I'm blind,' the words rang out, 'and likely to fall in the water without a hand to guide me. Go and fetch him!'

But this wasn't necessary; Torcal must have heard Rique and he came out from the shadowed doorway and walked towards them. He was tall and clad in a beige jacket and brown trousers; as he drew nearer Angie heard Maya catch her breath.

Angie saw instantly why that breathless sound had escaped from Maya. In the most uncanny way Torcal de Byas was the same lean, dark, noticeable sort of male that Rique was, except that he had intense blue eyes that were a striking contrast to his darkness. He rested them on her face, and then he looked at Maya, and for a fleeting moment their expression was tortured.

'Torcal?' Rique thrust out a hand, having caught the sound of masculine footfalls. 'How are you, *compadre*?'

'I'm fine.' The two men shook hands vigorously. 'You are looking much better yourself, Rique. If it wasn't for the cane I would think you could see across the water to Spain.'

'I wish to God it were so.' Rique was gazing directly at the other man because of his sense of direction; the scarring at the side of his face had become less raw and it was difficult to believe that the sunlight wasn't filtering into his eyes, whose mice-like gleams gave them an illusory radiance.

'Now let me introduce you to my companions,' Rique said. 'The brunette is my sister Maya, of whom you have heard me speak. The young blonde is my nurse, Angel Hart.'

'I'm glad to know you both.' Torcal de Byas had a

grave and charming smile, but once again Angie saw
the look of pain deep in his striking eyes; she knew
why it was there and when she caught Maya looking at
him with fascinated eyes she felt her heart sink.
Having just experienced a broken romance Maya was
vulnerable, and there was no indication that this man
whom she was meeting for the first time had suffered
an injury of a very grave nature. If Angie saw the rem-
nants of pain and shock in his lean face it was because she was a nurse, and Rique had confided in her
and would expect her to respect that confidence.

'You are fortunate, Rique,' Torcal glanced from one
girl to the other, 'to be in the hands of such charming
young women.'

'Do you know, Señor de Byas,' Maya smiled shyly
up at him, 'you are a very unusual Spaniard. Your
eyes are blue!'

'My mother was a Scot,' he explained. 'My father
met her while on a trip to Aberdeen to buy a stud bull.
Spanish bulls are excellent in the arena, but they
aren't always tender eating. He therefore introduced a
Scottish strain into his cattle and his family.'

'With success, I'm sure, *señor*,' Maya smiled.

'Please call me Torcal,' he said.

'I'd like that,' she rejoined. 'And you must call me
Maya.'

'An Aztec name; it suits you.' He glanced at Angie.
'I can see that you are a genuine Anglo-Saxon, Miss
Hart. Your hair gives you away; it really is blonde.'

When he said this, Maya gave Angie a rather sharp
look. 'Rique was telling us you met in hospital—were
you badly hurt, Torcal?'

'Quite seriously.' A nerve twitched in his jaw.

'And are you quite recovered?' she asked.

'Yes.' He said it rather curtly. 'I have made a re-servation at the Castelo de Madrigal; is it a good hotel?'

'Excellent,' said Rique. 'Now shall we go and eat? There used to be a rather interesting place we were fond of in our salad days, the Casa de las Palmas. I'm sure you'll approve my sister's choice, Torcal.'

'I should like you to be my guests——'

'Indeed not.' Rique spoke firmly. 'When a friend of mine visits Bayaltar for the first time, then I like to be the host. Angel, your arm, *por favor*.'

'*Si, señor*.' She gave Torcal a slight smile as she took Rique's hand and placed it in the crook of her arm. As they went up the steps to the street she could hear Maya getting acquainted with Torcal, and once again it crossed her mind that he was very attractive and Maya's bruised emotions were crying out to be soothed.

Lost in her thoughts, Angie stumbled on a step and Rique said reprovingly: 'I thought I was the one who can't see where I'm going.'

'Smart guy!' She gave a laugh, but inwardly she felt anxious; it probably hadn't crossed Rique's mind that his sister might feel attracted to the friend he had never seen. He didn't know that Torcal de Byas was like himself, the type of male to whom women were drawn.

'We might as well leave the car parked here and walk to the restaurant,' she said. 'It's situated in the plaza and that isn't far to walk.'

Rique jerked to a standstill. 'The Ramblas will be full of people at this time of the day!'

'So it will.' She held his hand firmly within the crook of her arm. 'You've got to get used to walking among people, *amigo*, so stop being neurotic about it.'

'You've about as much sympathy as a pincushion left in the middle of a chair,' he growled. 'For the love of heaven don't let me collide with anyone—we should be given a bell to wear, like the lepers used to have.'

'Don't be ridiculous,' she said. 'Anyway, that affliction stopped being contagious a long while ago and is now curable.'

'Unlike my affliction, eh?'

She glanced up at him with the sympathy she couldn't allow into her voice, and led him adroitly among the people hurrying along the narrow pavements of the Ramblas, either shopping or going to lunch, careless in the way of the sighted, unaware of the miracle of being surefooted and able to fend for themselves in a crowd.

Angie sensed that the hurrying feet and the sounds of traffic were assailing Rique's ears in a most confusing way; she knew that his nerves were stretched, but the restaurant was in sight and soon he would be sitting down with a drink.

'I never realised that people walked so quickly,' he said. 'They sound like a pack of elephants heading for the river.'

Angie gave a laugh, for a smile was lost on Rique. 'It's lunchtime for quite a few of them, so I hope we don't have to wait for a table.'

They arrived at the big plaza where café tables were set against tropical plants beneath gaily striped awnings. A marble fountain centred the plaza, its trio of basins spilling with sunlit sprays of water; at the far end there was a rococo bandstand and a pavilion bright with *azulejos*, the ornamental tiles that the Moors had taught the Latin people to use with such imagination.

To complete the picture were the tall palm trees whose graceful fronds were dark emerald against the sunshot sky.

'I like this,' Torcal said warmly. 'Rique, I had no idea your island was such a picturesque place.'

'It's unchanging, which is just as well in my case.' Rique's smile was a cynical twist of the lip. 'My father does his utmost to keep the island unspoiled by too much tourism. Imagine here the kind of hotels that have sprung up in parts of Spain. *Dios*, the last time I saw Ibiza—I didn't recognise it!'

'I look forward to meeting Don Carlos,' said Torcal as they made their way towards the Casa de las Palmas, with tables on its sidewalk and an arched entrance into the cool interior. Most of the outside tables were occupied, so they went inside where all sorts of coffee beans were sold along with various preserves, biscuits and breads.

'Heavenly smell, isn't it?' Maya had an eager light in her eyes as she looked up at Torcal. He smiled briefly in reply, the flame-coloured lamps of the restaurant giving his eyes a smoky tint as he glanced about for an unreserved table for four people. Fortunately there was one, set within one of the booths adorned by wrought-iron.

Angie glanced about her and her memories were tinged with a bitter-sweetness. Very little had changed and when she studied the menu she found upon it dishes she had enjoyed all those years ago, especially the fresh sardines grilled over charcoal, with crusty bread and butter.

'Now, what is everyone drinking?' Rique wanted to know. 'I fancy a Bacardi rum myself, a nice tall one.'

'Pisco sour for me,' said Torcal.

'Does it taste sour?' Maya wanted to know.

A smile glimmered in his eyes. 'It's a nice shade of green.'

'Do you think I'd like it, Torcal?' She spoke his name with soft hesitancy, Angie noticed, as if she sensed something about him that warned a woman he was not as approachable as other men.

'You could try it,' he told her, 'but I should think Sangria would be more to your taste.'

'What is my taste?' she asked him, a slight flush giving her skin that underglow of a girl on the breathless brink of excitement. Angie saw it and was glad that Rique was unaware . . . though allowance had to be made for the fact that his hearing was finely attuned to the rhythms of the voice.

'You're very young,' Torcal said indulgently. 'The sweet things of life have not yet turned sour for you.'

'That's all you know.' Maya's red mouth sulked for a moment and it was obvious she was thinking of the young singer her father had denied her.

'I'd like Sangria,' said Angie. 'Aren't Spanish words attractive? Think how much nicer *ramblas* sounds than main street.'

'It's true,' Torcal agreed. 'You have very little accent—I may call you Angie, may I not?'

'Of course,' she agreed. 'I learned my Spanish when I used to come to Bayaltar as a schoolgirl.'

'Then you—ah, I see.' Torcal slid into silence as the

waiter came to the table and hovered over Rique, whose white cane was the folding type which had been placed on the banquette which he shared with Angie.

'And what would the *señor* like to order?' the waiter enquired.

Rique looked at him with his uncanny directness, and Angie could see that it pleased him that the waiter took him for a sighted man. He ordered their various drinks while Torcal watched him with grave blue eyes, making Angie wonder if he was weighing his own disability against Rique's world without colours or faces or the pleasure of seeing someone smile. Abruptly his eyes were upon Angie's face, searching it, as if suddenly the suspicion stabbed that Rique might have told her what had happened to him.

'In which part of Spain do you live?' she asked him, keeping her face politely composed.

'I have a flat in Madrid,' he said. 'My people live down in Andalusia where they have a sizeable *estancia*.'

'I've heard that Andalusia is very beautiful and not quite so spoiled as the coastal parts of Spain.'

'It's lost in time,' he agreed, 'much like this island. The Moorish influence remains strong and adds that touch of mystery; hot white sunlight and the cool sound of fountains, black shadows and veiled women.'

'Do you like veiled women?' Maya asked him.

'As part of the scenery. What is your opinion, Rique?'

'These days,' Rique drawled, 'all women wear veils as far as I'm concerned.'

'Ah, I didn't mean—*perdón*!' Torcal looked pained by his own thoughtlessness.

'Give it no more thought, *amigo*. I like people to forget that I'm blind, so just keep doing it.'

'Do you have to go back to hospital after your holiday?' Maya gazed at Torcal as if the fascination of his blue eyes had almost made her forget that she had recently claimed to be in love. She had an elbow propped on the table and her chin cupped in the palm of her hand and she seemed lost in his eyes.

'No, they have done all they can for me.' There was a note of quiet irony in his voice.

'They've made you better?' Maya looked anxious. 'You look fine.'

'I feel fine.' And he looked relieved as the waiter brought their drinks and placed them on the table. 'Ah good, I have a thirst.'

With her tactful casualness Angie placed Rique's drink in his hand. '*Salud*.' He raised the glass to his lips and took a deep swallow. 'How's the Sangria?'

'Delicious.' It really was, being a combination of red wine, cognac, soda water, slices of orange, lemon juice, slithers of pineapple and cracked ice.

During lunch the two men talked about their varied experiences, and Angie noticed that Maya listened intently to the conversation, as if she wanted to learn all she could about this man who had entered her life so unexpectedly.

Dear heaven, Angie thought, Rique's sister was heading for real problems if she became infatuated with Torcal de Byas. Even if he found her appealing in return he couldn't offer her a normal relationship, and Angie doubted if Rique would encourage such an attachment without telling his father what it entailed for Maya. She would never experience lovemaking that would result in children, and though it was obvious that Rique found Torcal a congenial friend, he had it in him to ruthlessly end that friendship if he thought his sister might fall in love with Torcal.

He was deeply passionate at the core of him and would regard passion as important to a woman as to a man, and Angie couldn't imagine him allowing Maya to be deprived of the warmth and excitement of being fully possessed by the man she married.

Angie sighed quietly and squeezed lemon juice on to the pancake she had chosen for dessert. As delicious as lunch had been she couldn't shake off a feeling of depression, and then she wondered if Rique sensed her mood, for he asked Torcal to beckon the waiter and when he came to the table Rique ordered some more of the wine whose *solera madre*, he said, was a warm and heartening one.

'We'll all go out of here tipsy,' Maya laughed. 'I haven't seen you like this for a long time, Rique. Do we give the credit to Angie or the wine?'

'Well, Angel,' he turned towards her, 'what do you think of your patient? Do you think the credit is due to you?'

'I would say so,' Torcal looked across at Angie with that slightly sad smile in his vivid eyes. 'My nurse was nothing like yours, Rique. She was almost six feet tall and well in proportion, a real dragon.'

'I sometimes think Rique deserves a dragon,' said Maya, 'the way he treats Angie at times. I've often heard her in his room in the small hours reading a book to him.'

'Why not?' Rique weaved his wine glass back and forth beneath his nose, breathing the bouquet of the sun-coloured wine. 'We have a sizeable collection of novels in the house; my mother loved them and I must say I find their pure escapism easy on the ear. What is the peculiar title of the one we are on at the present time, Angel?'

'*The Bitter Tea of General Yen*.' Angie smiled and fondled the stem of her wine glass. 'I'm enjoying the story myself, it's rather unusual and very romantic.'

'Are you a romantic person?' Torcal asked her.

'I—I suppose I have my fair share of romanticism, though it's rather out of fashion these days, isn't it? Modern books, plays and films would have us grappling with reality twenty-four hours a day, and that,' she said wryly, 'can be a little hard on nurses. I enjoy a book or a film which helps me to forget about the pain and indignity of illness, but I suppose as a journalist you prefer the realistic view of life?'

'Do I?' Torcal's blue eyes were reflective. 'I did a lot of thinking while I was laid up in hospital and I started to wonder if I should go back to Andalusia and the land. My father grows older and he would like to slacken his hold on the reins if I should be willing to take them; it's many years since my mother smelled Scottish heather, so I might decide to get soil on my hands instead of ink.'

'It sounds like a good idea,' Rique approved. 'You could always return to the pen if the plough proved heavy going. Believe me, I wish I had an alternative to whittling clothes pegs and selling them.'

'Rique, I do hate it when you talk in that way,' Maya exclaimed. 'You have become such a cynic.'

'Perhaps.' He shrugged. 'But there aren't many avenues for a blind man to explore, are there?'

'You could do as Angie suggested and study law.'

'And how do I read up on it?' he asked. 'I doubt if they put law books into Braille.'

'There's a chance that many of them are on tape,' Angie suggested. 'We could find out——'

'Please yourself,' he said offhandedly. 'I can't say I'm all that interested—now, has everybody had a satisfying lunch?'

'It was superb,' Torcal said warmly. 'Your island air is certainly good for the appetite. I haven't eaten chocolate cake with inch-thick vanilla cream since I was a boy.'

'It was delicious, wasn't it?' Maya had persuaded him to try the cake, a speciality of the *casa* among the palms. She cradled her wine glass and gazed at Torcal as if silently begging him to find her as sweet as he had found the cake.

Angie's fingers gripped the stem of her wine glass very tightly; she was in no doubt that Maya was falling under the spell of those Celtic blue eyes and the charm of a man older than herself. Angie could understand the attraction because it had happened to herself with regard to Rique, but she had her career to fall back on when this sojourn with him was over and hard work in some English hospital would ensure that she found little time to brood.

She lifted her wine glass and took a deep swallow ... she didn't want to think about leaving Rique ... she wished time could stand still and all four of them could always be as they were right now, as they sat talking in the relaxed atmosphere of the *casa*.

But even as she thought this, Rique asked her to beckon the waiter so he could settle the bill.

'Allow me to do the honours.' Torcal beckoned the waiter. 'This has been the kind of meal that helps one to forget—problems.'

'Then if you wish.' Rique didn't argue the point, and if something in the way Torcal spoke had made Maya curious, she leaned to him and laid a hand on his. It was as if she wanted to comfort him without really knowing why.

'How long will you be staying on the island?' she asked.

'I—haven't made any definite plans.'

'I know every inch of the island, Torcal, so you must let me show you around. It's an interesting place and we have a beach close to the Residencia. Do you like to swim?'

'No!' He removed his hand from beneath hers. 'I don't mind sailing, but I don't swim.'

'But it's great fun—surely you learned as a boy?'

'I learned,' he said, 'but it isn't an activity I'm keen on.'

'Maya, stop being a pest.' Rique spoke with a slight edge to his voice. 'Torcal has come to Bayaltar to recuperate, so allow him to choose his own diversions—they might not include your guided tours.'

'I—I'm sorry if I'm being a pest——' Sudden tears swam into Maya's eyes and she jumped to her feet and pushed past Torcal. 'Excuse me, I—I'm going to the ladies' room. Are you coming, Angie?'

They made their way to the washroom and Maya said resentfully: 'I don't think there was any need for Rique to speak like that to me because I asked Torcal if he would like me to show him the island. Did I seem as if I was throwing myself at his head?'

'Not to me,' Angie soothed. 'It's just that your brother's aware of what his friend has been through and that his nerves are still shaken.'

A few minutes later when they stood at the mirrors repairing their make-up Maya said softly: 'He's so attractive, *tiene gracia*. His eyes send tingles up and down my spine—what is your opinion of him?'

'Charming but enigmatic,' Angie replied. 'Be cautious, Maya. You may be feeling the effects of a rebound from what you felt for——'

'No,' Maya shook her head and gazed thoughtfully at Angie's reflection. 'It's all over with him—he was shallow compared to Torcal. He's a real man and he's deep as the sea, isn't he?'

'Yes, he's certainly that,' Angie agreed. 'You've lived by the sea all your life, Maya, so you know you have to respect it.'

'Meaning that there's something unpredictable about Torcal?' Maya turned to face Angie, something a little wilful showing in her eyes.

'There are some people you have to take care with.'

'You think he's rather like Rique?'

'He and Rique have been hurt in ways that can be damaging.'

'Rique is blinded and I understand his bitterness, but Torcal—anyone can see that he's made a good recovery from his injuries. If he has scars, they aren't visible ones.'

'No,' Angie said quietly. 'Scars aren't always visible, but that doesn't mean they aren't there.'

'Angie, what has Rique told you about Torcal? He has said something, hasn't he, and it's something serious. Was Torcal very badly hurt?'

'I—believe so.'

'I believe you know all about it, but you aren't going to tell me! Why not, Angie? Do you fancy Torcal yourself?'

Angie caught her breath. 'For heaven's sake, Maya, one day you're pining for a guitarist and the next you're imagining yourself in love with a man you've only just met! It takes a bit longer than that to fall in love; it goes beyond that immediate sense of attraction.'

'Are you speaking from experience?' Maya's dark eyes held a flash of jealousy. 'Are you in love?'

'I've had enough of this conversation.' Angie walked to the door and was about to open it when Maya gripped her arm with tense fingers.

'We used to tell each other everything, but these days you're so secretive, Angie, as if being a nurse makes you more adult. Why should you know things that I don't know?'

'If you want to be treated like an adult, then behave like one,' Angie retorted. 'Torcal de Byas is certainly attractive, but he's been through a traumatic experience and I don't imagine he came to Bayaltar with the intention of getting emotionally involved with anyone. Don't rush him, Maya. He has to come to terms with—with himself.'

'What is it you're not telling me?' Maya demanded. 'Is he divorced?'

'No—his wife was killed in an accident a few months after their marriage.'

'Sweet Jesus!' Maya crossed herself. 'No wonder I sense that he pushes people away from him and yet in his heart wishes them to come close. Poor Torcal, he must be afraid to let himself be happy in case he has to face misery again. I—I'd love to help him——'

'Maya, don't let youself be hurt again.' Angie looked at her friend in a worried way. 'Torcal's good-looking, but all that's happened to him is too close to the surface and still hurting him.'

'There's something about him that touches me on a nerve, just here.' Maya touched herself just under her rib cage. 'He looks at me with those eyes and I quiver—that's never happened to me before. Do you know what I mean, Angie?'

'Of course I know,' Angie spoke feelingly, 'but don't let the feeling fool you. He's been wounded and you're bound to feel touched by him—as I do about your brother.'

'You knew Rique when we were young, so you're more like a sister to him. You're like a member of the family almost.'

'Yes—perhaps.' The admission hurt because never for a moment with Rique did Angie feel like his sister; when his hand rested in the crook of her arm the rest of her body was aware of his touch. When he sank into a bitter mood no one knew how hard she fought to prise him out of it again. His every ache and fear was hers; she was so attuned to his needs that she would wake in the night and know that he lay awake in the darkness that a lamp couldn't lighten and she would slip into her dressing-gown and go down to the kitchen to make him a warm drink, sometimes milk with a slug of rum in it and a spoonful of butter. When the nightcap sent him off to sleep no one was aware that she often spent the remainder of the night in the arm-chair beside his bed, her feet in his slippers for warmth and some kind of consolation.

'I suppose you think I'm fickle,' said Maya. 'I suppose you're the sort to go on loving a man even if he did let you down.'

'If it's love we're talking about and not a fantasy.' Angie looked directly at Maya. 'Love isn't a magic key that lets us into a land of romance and rapture; sometimes it demands a tolerance and a tenderness of a very special kind. I don't think you're fickle, Maya, but I do believe you have a romantic imagination and you see Torcal as the handsome hero rather than a man whose emotions as well as his body have been torn about.'

'So you're telling me not to get romantic about him, is that it, Angie?'

'I'm advising you——'

'I don't want your advice!' A stormy light seethed in Maya's eyes as they swept Angie up and down. 'You like him yourself and you think you can frighten me off with your hints and innuendoes. I saw you looking at him as we ate lunch—to think that after all these years we should start falling out over a man! I don't want to fall out with you, Angie, but where Torcal's concerned you can mind your own business!'

'Very well,' Angie said quietly, 'I'll do that, but don't come running to Rique if something should happen and you find yourself—hurt in some way.'

'What are you implying?' Maya stormed. 'Are you suggesting that Torcal is—violent?'

'No.'

'Then what is it about him that makes you hint things? I want to know, so tell me!'

'It isn't my place to do so——'

'Rique knows, doesn't he? I shall ask him——'

'You will do nothing of the sort!' Sudden anger shook Angie. 'You've grown up into a spoiled girl, Maya, and you want everything you fancy like a kid in a pastry shop. These are two men who have been through such hell as you can't even imagine, so don't pester Rique, and let Torcal alone if he chooses to be that way. Start being a woman!'

Maya gazed at Angie with her mouth ajar, as if the words she wanted to say were struck motionless by Angie's unexpected flare of temper. 'I see what's the matter,' she said at last, 'it's Rique you're so concerned about. It's Rique, and I—I believe you're crazy about him!'

'I'm a nurse and he's my patient.' Angie pulled herself together and dropped her lipstick into her bag, avoiding Maya's eyes. 'He's making progress and I don't want him worried—he will worry if he thinks you want to get romantic about Torcal.'

'You've gone and got romantic about my brother, haven't you?' Suddenly Maya reached out and caught at Angie's hand, holding it over the clasp of her bag. 'I don't know why I didn't guess beforehand. No one could be as devoted as you are to him and not be in love with him. When I phoned to ask if you could come and be his nurse you didn't hesitate for a second and I thought you were coming as a token of friendship, but all the time—Angie, I don't know what to say. Does he know?'

Angie shook her head. 'He mustn't know, Maya, so please promise me never to say a word.'

'But why mustn't he know?'

'Because if he gets well, I am not the girl for him.

No more, Maya, than Torcal de Byas is the man for you.'

'You seem so certain about that.' Maya seemed to droop a little. 'Do you think he's still in love with his dead wife?'

Angie nodded, for this was the easiest way to mislead Maya and it could well be true that Torcal still loved the girl he had lost so early in his marriage.

'Is that what Rique thinks?' Maya persisted.

'Yes. Shall we go now? They'll be wondering what has become of us.'

'Angie, I wish I was as strong as you.'

Angie smiled slightly. 'It comes with practice and, please, what we have said in this room has been in strict confidence. Whatever I feel for your brother is my concern.'

'Angie, why aren't you the girl for him? Just tell me that.'

'Because he's the son of Carlos de Zaldo and your father will want him to marry a girl of Spanish blood. Added to which,' Angie infused a casual note into her voice, though it took some doing, 'your brother has never shown the slightest romantic interest in me; I was never his type. You see, Maya, I am trapped for always by his visual memory of me as a schoolgirl in plaits. Could you expect a man of the world like Rique to—to be in love with that image? Every day he gets more certain in his handling of his blindness and his health is improving. One day soon, apart from his lack of sight, he will be the upright, confident, rather arrogant Rique he always was. My job will then be over and I shall say *Vaya con Dios* and return to my own country.

'Some things, you see, have to be the way they are

meant to be. We can't twist them to suit our purpose—don't imagine that Rique's reliance upon me hasn't suggested itself as an easy way to get him. He turns to me in the night when he can't sleep and I could have made myself indispensable to him in that way—had I chosen to.'

'Instead you chose *The Bitter Tea of General Yen*.' Suddenly tears swam in Maya's eyes and in the quick emotional way of their schooldays she flung her arms about Angie's neck and kissed the silky skin of her cheek. 'I—I'm glad we're friends again.'

'So am I. Now let's rejoin the men before Rique sends someone to fetch us.'

Maya gave a shaky laugh and brushed away a tear. 'You know him so well, don't you?'

'Too well,' Angie said drily, the dull ache at the base of her throat a warning that it would be all too easy to break into tears of her own.

'Surely it wouldn't hurt if I invited Torcal to do a little sightseeing? I promise not to make a nuisance of myself.' Maya's large Spanish eyes were beseeching. 'I do understand about what he's been through; that's part of why I like him. I want to help him forget.'

For Torcal, as Angie knew, there was to be no forgetting, and if she read the man with clear vision then she knew he would invite no young and vibrant young woman to fall in love with him.

'Be his friend,' Angie urged, 'as I am Rique's. Accept that it may be all that he will ask of you.'

'If he should ask more, is there some terrible reason why I should refuse him?'

'There may be,' Angie said cautiously.

'All right.' Maya firmed her shoulders. 'I shall live

for each day, as you do, Angie, and I shan't ask for the moon if I'm only meant to have a handful of stars. If that's being grown up, then I am.'

They rejoined the men and quite casually Maya invited Torcal to take a stroll with her. She added that she would show him the nearby mosque and the bazaar. 'You will think you are in Morocco.'

'Then how can I resist?' He very lightly touched Rique's sleeve. 'Do you mind, *amigo*, if I permit your sister to be my guide for an hour?'

'By all means,' Rique rejoined, 'allow her to be your guide.'

Torcal inclined his head, though Rique couldn't see that he did so with the resignation of a man who heard the undercurrent of warning in Rique's voice.

'*Gracias*, Rique.'

They walked away, a tall, lean man bending his dark head to listen to the remarks of the brightly clad girl at his side.

'Angie,' Rique spoke in a sombre voice, 'Maya can't be allowed to get ideas about Torcal. I hope he understands.'

'I'm sure he does, Rique.' She hesitated a moment. 'But would it be so bad if they fell for each other?'

'No man,' he said harshly, 'has the right to love a woman if he can't give her the whole of love. I don't just say that for him, I say it for myself. I don't sit in judgment on Torcal and exclude my own limitations as a blind man. If a woman is worth loving then she is worth all and every part of a man ... love demands that it be all or nothing!'

Angie gazed at Rique's adamant face, its every feature carved and bold in the sunlight, the sun itself streaming into eyes that didn't blink as hers did.

They looked into the empty darkness and couldn't see the love that drained her face to a fragile pallor. What, she wondered, would she be risking if she told him she loved him? Would he call her a fool and thrust her away from him? Would he ask his father to send her away because she had become an embarrassment?

Or would he accept her offer on the basis that you could only truly hurt the one whom you truly loved?

The temptation took her by the throat . . . she knew of his needs and her own longings. She knew, also, that Rique believed he was going to die in the near future, and it was a dread possibility which had to be faced. But whether or not she would have declared her feelings as they stood there in the brazen sunlight of the plaza was to remain a mystery.

'Rique, by all that's holy!'

The figure that loped across the plaza was a well-built, handsome one, clad in a white suit that offset his looks. He clapped a hand on Rique's shoulder and his dark eyes were sparkling.

'Brother, I expected to find you an invalid, but here you are and it's a sheer marvel! No one wrote to tell me you had got back your sight!'

'Seb!' The name came faintly from Angie; she felt an emotional draining that almost made her feel faint.

'Seb?' Rique spoke the name in a stronger voice. 'Is that you?'

Sebastian de Zaldo stood there gazing at his brother and slowly the pleasure ebbed from his eye. He glanced at Angie and she shook her head.

'By the saints——' Seb took a deep breath, then flung both arms about his brother. 'You're looking good, Rique.'

'I'm looking at you, *mi hermano*,' Rique's smile was

a twist of the lip, 'but I am only guessing that you are as handsome as ever. How come you suddenly turn up? Did you arrive on the launch?'

'No.' Seb was looking closely at his brother, as if still unable to believe there was no light in his eyes when they looked so alive. 'I came in the Company helicopter and I've just finished having lunch with the pilot, who has now flown back to Madrid. Rique, you are looking incredibly fit, and it's damnably hard to believe that you can't——'

'That I'm blind?' Rique had never looked more sardonic. 'You will have to get used to the word, brother, because it's going to be around as long as I am.'

'I——' Seb's hand clenched his brother's shoulder, 'I don't know what to say, old man.'

'Then don't say anything, Seb, just accept it.'

'You have seen the very best consultants?'

'They have seen me,' Rique drawled. 'Would Padre have it otherwise? Now tell me something—how pretty is this nurse of mine?'

Seb smiled slightly and ran his eyes over Angie's slim figure in the cool cream dress, a slender chain about her neck matching her gold hair. A truant lock of hair was adrift on her brow, adding an endearing air of disarray to her otherwise neat appearance.

'Pretty isn't the word,' Seb informed his brother, and his eyes stayed upon Angie as he spoke. 'She's very lovely—I thought so in London and I'm convinced now I see her back on the island.'

'I'm glad she's lovely.' Rique said it very quietly. 'You and she, Seb, must make a good match—what a pity I can't see you side by side.'

Something wailed inside Angie when he said those words . . . she wanted to fling herself at him, to cling

and hold him safe from the brink of the pit he felt at
his feet each time he took a step in the dark.

'Rique,' her heart cried out in its own silent darkness, 'Rique, I want only you . . . you for always, or
never!'

CHAPTER SEVEN

ANGIE drank cool lemon tea with mint and ice added,
seated beneath the bauhinia tree on the shady side of
the patio. The orchid-like flowers were a deep purple
and nearby there was a fern-tree, its stem as graceful
as a slim lady in a green gown with a trailing hem.
Through the foliage and below the plateau on which
stood the Casera de Nusta spangles of light danced
across the sea.

House of the Sun Virgin, the name given to it by the
very first Carlos de Zaldo to take up residence after
returning from successful voyages as a Captain in the
larcenous navy of King Philip of Spain. He had
brought with him a bride from across the seas, a half-
wild Peruvian girl for whom the house had been named.

From that alliance had sprung the present-day
Zaldo men, each in his way an individual of dignified
charm and a dash of steel that was never quite concealed.

These men represented for Angie all that was dash-
ing and brave, and admittedly chauvinistic in the character of the Spanish male.

Even Sebastian, the brother who had ventured into
the commercial world of cinematic art, had upon his
return to the island resumed his look of being de-

scended from *conquistadores* in high leather boots, steel armour and the arrogance of the Golden Age when Drake of England had been commissioned by the first Elizabeth to conquer and subdue the galleons of the Armada. His success had been a mixed one; his tactics might have sunk a number of the galleons, but still strong in the Spaniard was the hauteur and pride of the old days. He believed strongly in family loyalty and closeness, and this trait was still very much alive in Sebastian.

He had decided that Rique should attempt some of his old sporting pursuits such as riding, sea-fishing and perhaps some archery.

'You've got to be as crazy as those characters you work with in films,' Rique had said. 'How do I see to guide the horse, and where do I aim my arrows?'

'You learn, brother,' Seb had said. 'You practise, and who cares a curse if you don't hit the target. You'll be participating—doesn't the thought of it excite you?'

Rique had smiled slowly, and Angie's heart had beaten fast with eagerness for him to agree.

'Very well,' he had drawled. 'I must say I'd sooner break my neck from a saddle than die in bed.'

He had worn what Angie called his Gustave Doré face as he spoke, and she would never forget the stricken look Seb had flung at her. '*Christos*, I could clout you across the chin when you talk that way,' he had shouted. 'No blasted piece of terrorist bomb is going to kill you, Rique. You've got to believe it!'

'You believe it for me,' Rique had said. 'You and Angel.'

The ice tinkled in Angie's lemon tea as she raised it

to her lips. The flowers of the bauhinia moved languidly in a soft breeze rising off the sea and there was a soft tinkle of eucalyptus leaves as small bright birds flitted among them. Her gaze stole around the patio and rested upon the *atalaya* that cast its slim shadow down upon the tiles.

Since Seb's homecoming Rique had consistently paired them. 'Why don't you and Angel take a walk to the beach?' he'd say. 'Why don't you go into town for the evening?'

'Please, Rique!' she would protest. 'I'm sure your brother can find his own companion.'

But Seb seemed genuinely to want her company, and Angie had to admit it was balm upon the wound caused by Rique when he thrust her away from him on to his brother. Seb was a charmer, with not an ounce of conceit in him. They danced at the El Morocco, and sailed around the island in the *Catalina*, his father's sloop. He made no secret of his liking for her, while Angie held her own secret tucked away in her heart. She felt sure she could trust Maya, who slipped in and out of the Residencia with an absorbed look in her eyes. She told no one that she was seeing Torcal, but it was obvious to Angie that she spent a good deal of time with him. Once he had dined at the house and Don Carlos had seemed impressed by him. Rique hadn't said anything, but Angie had noticed the hard set set to his jaw. She knew he liked Torcal; he wouldn't find it easy having to tell his friend that Maya deserved what he had called the whole of love. He would be as ruthless with Torcal as he was with himself.

Angie sat there, slim legs stretched out upon the

springy bamboo slats of the lounging chair. She was lost in her thoughts as bees plundered the nearby flowers; she heard nothing but the things Rique had said: felt nothing but the pain and pleasure it had given her to be with him these past few weeks.

She sighed and wished there was a cure for love, but like most deep-seated ailments it had a way of getting worse instead of better, and only by cutting herself off from the cause would she eventually find peace of body and mind.

'So quiet, fair lady, so lost in dreams.'

She glanced round and there was Seb leaning against the bauhinia tree, clad in gaucho trousers and a dark blue shirt, a thin cigar clamped between his teeth.

Her eyes dwelt upon his face as her thoughts came to order. There was a disturbing kindness in his ebony dark eyes above the bold family nose; he was like Rique except that everything about him was cast in a less rugged mould, nor was his skin such a deep shade of brown. When Rique looked at a woman, even with his blind eyes, there was something dangerous about him.

That thread of danger had not been woven into Seb's nature and it was true what Rique said about him; he was that much nicer, not the sort of man to serve as a soldier from choice, and kill because it was a necessary evil in a world where force was often brutish and cruel.

'Your fairness always startles me.' He withdrew the cigar from his lips and smiled slowly. 'It goes all the way through, doesn't it, and isn't just silver-gold plating? I've seen so much artificiality in the past few years that looking at you, Angie, is soothing and cool.'

'Do you enjoy your work?' she asked, accepting his compliment with a coolness that wouldn't have been possible had Rique made it. The very thought of Rique paying her such a compliment made her nerves flutter, but the nearest he came to flattery was to tell her she was the least intrusive female he had met ... which seemed a backhanded way of telling her she made little impression upon him.

'Sometimes,' Seb told her, 'I achieve something that gives me a good feeling. Much the way you must feel when you can help someone the way you've helped Rique.'

'What I've had to do,' she said, 'is to help Rique to help himself. He has a perceptive mind and it's in his fingers as well, that's one of the reasons he's making such rapid progress with his Braille.'

'He's still very bitter, isn't he?' Seb's face became sombre. 'While we were out riding I remarked on the good feeling the sun gives a person—"Midnight, sunlight, what the hell?" he replied. "It's all the same to me!" I got all choked up, do you know that, Angie? It comes hard to him because he's always been a man of action. He was one heck of a good soldier. Not my line, but certainly Rique's. He'd have gone right to the top—now, poor devil, he feels right at the bottom— and, God, it must be dark down there! I don't know that I could stand it.'

'He has to, Seb. He has to learn to live with it.'

Seb held the gravity of Angie's gaze. 'He doesn't think he's going to make it, does he? What has the doctor said to you about him and his chances?'

'Dr Romaldo has been candid about Rique's case. There are metal fragments embedded and they could

cause some kind of an infection, or even shift and———'
She moved her hands in an eloquent gesture. 'Some
patients are willing to push such things to the back of
the mind, but Rique is so very forthright and trained
to face the enemy.'

'He can't be an easy patient for you, Angie.' A tinge
of curiosity came into Seb's eyes. 'How do you cope
when he's in one of his forthright moods?'

'Sometimes with difficulty,' she smiled. 'I'm glad
you've persuaded him to take up riding again. I'm not
so sure about the archery.'

'If you're used to his verbal slings and arrows,
Angie, then it should be easy enough to stand clear of
the ones he lets fly from a bowstring. He used to be a
good shot—do you remember?'

She nodded. 'There's very little I've forgotten about
my holidays on Bayaltar. I used to love them.'

'We had a lot of fun, didn't we?' His smile was nos-
talgic. 'When we are young we take no heed of "time's
winged chariot", do we?'

'None at all,' she agreed. 'When we look back upon
summers gone they seem always to have been sunny
ones.'

'It was good of you to come when my father
called—God, but it's hit him hard. Rique was always
special to him, as the eldest son is in the household of
a Spaniard; but apart from that they had—have a lot in
common. There I go, thinking of Rique in the past
tense, as if the Rique who is blind is a different
person.'

'He is in a way,' said Angie. 'It's coming to terms
with that which makes him snarl at times; he can't
stride out as he used to because there might be

something in his path; he can't judge people from their looks or manner, so he has to let his ears do the work for him. He has become a deeper person, Seb, because he has had to become a more deliberate one.'

'You admire him, don't you, Angie?'

'Of course.' Her heart gave a nervous leap. 'I think he's very brave.'

'And what do you think of me, *querida*?'

It wasn't the first time Seb had called her darling, nor the first time she had seen him looking at her as if he wanted to take her into his arms. Why, she wondered, did her heart yearn for Rique when she meant so little to him as a woman? Seb was equally attractive and much kinder, and there was no mistaking the beckoning look in his eyes.

Suddenly he came to her, sat down on the end of the lounger and leaned towards her. 'Your eyes fascinate me,' he said softly. 'They have changing lights in them, do you know it? They have a self-dreaming quality and I like the way shadow and gaiety come and go in them. I like your haughty little English nose . . . and your kiss-starved mouth.'

'Seb . . .' She caught her breath. 'Don't say these things!'

'Why not?' he asked. 'I mean them and you are free to hear them. Don't you like the look of me? I'm not too bad, am I?'

'You're very good-looking.'

'I'm also kind to animals—I actually dislike the bullfight, much to the disdain of my brother. Are you the kind of girl who needs to have a man prove his *machismo*?'

She shook her head. 'I'm employed here as a

nurse—you shouldn't——'

'You must have known when we were kids that I liked you, Angie. Now when I look at you I have to do this.' He reached forward and drew his hands down her pale shining hair. 'You grew up exactly the way I knew you would.'

'With no surprises?' She smiled slightly.

'With several, as a matter of fact. You have some mystery about you—I'm with you right now and yet I feel that you aren't really with me. I wish I could read your mind.'

He pressed his hands to her brow and gazed deep in her eyes. 'Dreams move through the mind like phantom fish in a bowl, what are your dreams, Angie? You go quietly and efficiently about your work, so self-contained that sometimes you are maddening. You are gentle and caring, and yet there is a flame smouldering in you that I should like to fan into hot life. That time in London you said there was no special man in your life; does that still hold true?'

'There's no man I expect to—to share my life with,' she agreed.

'What made you trip over those words?' he demanded, a sudden flare to his nostrils that made him look like Rique.

'Did I?' She strove not to evade his eyes; evasion would increase his curiosity about her. 'I'm not used to being quizzed about my private life.'

'You're a very private person, aren't you, *querida*?'

'Yes, and I don't think you should get into the habit of calling me—that.'

'Darling?'

'You might go and say it in front of your father.'

'You think my father would disapprove of his second son falling in love with an English girl?'

'Yes—and you mustn't talk about—love.'

'Love is one of the nicest things to talk about—and to make.' He leaned closer and suddenly his lips were touching hers. It was a kiss which sought a response rather than demanded one, and because he was Seb and they had known and liked each other in those long and laughing days of summer she let his lips linger on hers. She didn't resist when he enfolded her in his arms and moved his lips down the side of her neck.

'Sweet,' he murmured. 'You smell of an English garden when the lavender stalks are heavy with seed. You aren't going to get away from me!'

'Please, Seb——' She didn't struggle or resist but was in a sudden panic at the way he was showing his feelings . . . with any man but Seb it would have been easy to ask for her release in the undesiring voice that could so readily cool the ardour in men, but he was Rique's brother and she wasn't a girl who found it easy to hurt people who meant something to her.

He pressed his cheek to her hair and his lips toyed with the lobe of the ear nearest to his mouth. 'I know the kind of girl you are,' he murmured. 'You are sensuous and yet aloof; you are cool because you are a little afraid of being warm: you protect your own integrity and I admire that beyond anything. Angie, *querida*, I want you very much, but I'm not going to rush your defences. I just want to let you know how I feel so you can think about it.'

'Seb——' She trembled slightly, aware that it lowered her defences to have a man so attractive and so protective talking to her in this way and holding her close to the vital warmth of his body. The radiation of his warmth after the rather brusque distance in Rique's manner was very hard to resist . . . like coming in from the cold and finding a glowing fire to welcome her.

'I always admired your hair, Angie.' Seb's lips brushed through it.

'I thought Spaniards liked women to have long hair as a symbol of their enslavement.' She tried to speak lightly.

'You had long hair, *niña mia*, so you could grow it again.'

'Long hair is a nuisance under a nurse's cap,' she rejoined.

'I should want you to give up nursing. I should want you to myself so I could love you and love you.'

'Love?' she murmured. 'What is love?'

'An opening of the heart—a hurricane of the emotions.'

'It sounds very elemental.'

'The most elemental thing that can happen to us that we can enjoy. You must have given some thought to falling in love, *querida*.'

'A nurse is kept very busy so that when she falls into bed she falls asleep and has little time for mooning.'

'Is that what the English call it, mooning? What an unromantic race of people you pretend to be! Why do the English hide themselves behind a mask of reserve?'

'I suppose because it's our way. The Spanish are like the palm tree, but we are like the oak. The palm tree flaunts its stem and waves its fronds at the world, but the oak cloaks itself in leaves. We are what we are, Seb.'

'I wouldn't have you any different from what you

are.' He tilted her chin and searched her eyes. 'What makes you think my father would disapprove if I chose to marry an English girl?'

'He's Spanish to his backbone and I think he'd want his three children to marry persons of Spanish blood.'

'He might expect that of Rique,' Seb said thoughtfully, 'but fortunately I'm not the eldest son—unless the unthinkable should happen and Rique should die. But he won't—he won't, will he, Angie?'

Rejection of it screamed through Angie's skull; how would she go on living and breathing if Rique should cease to be? How would it be possible for anything to matter any more? It would be hard enough to bear that he would be living a life she couldn't share, but at least she would know he was alive, smiling that wry twist of a smile, hating that white stick that must guide him through his black world, but upright all the same and feeling the island sun warm on his skin.

'A nurse is trained to think only in positive terms,' she said quietly. 'All being well Rique could live another fifty years.'

'God willing.' Seb crossed himself.

'None of us know our fate, Seb. I could die tomorrow; no one hands out guarantees on our life span.'

'I know my fate,' he said a trifle arrogantly, a smouldering look in his eyes as they swept over her. 'Apart from which there is this *musica y danza* which my father insists upon throwing in my honour. He has never quite come to terms with the way I earn my living, but I am home for a while, so he wants the fatted calf roasted under the Chinese lanterns, washed down with plenty of wine. It should be fun. Do you suppose Maya will invite this fellow she's been seeing? What do you make of him?'

'He's rather charming,' she said cautiously.

'I'm sorry I wasn't dining at home the evening he came here. I understand from Aunt Francisca that he's quite a few years older than Maya—is that a disadvantage in your opinion, Angie, or do you like the idea of a man being more experienced?'

'I can't speak for Maya,' she fenced. 'I shouldn't think there's anything lasting in her friendship with Torcal; it will no doubt peter out when he leaves Bayaltar.'

'Yet she seems rather intense and wrapped up in her thoughts—you say he's a charmer?'

'Not in the sense that he's a practised one; he's not that sort of a man. He's—interesting, and as you say, rather older than Maya, and so he's able to hold her interest.'

'I'd say he's made quite an impression on her.' Seb spoke thoughtfully. 'Girls are inclined to moon, aren't they, when they fall in love? You called it mooning.'

'I hope——' Angie bit her lip. 'Torcal's a widower and it might not be very wise of Maya to—care for him.'

'You think his heart is buried with his wife?'

'Yes.'

'We know that happens, Angie, when someone special dies, but life has to go on and Maya might make the fellow happy—why do you seem doubtful? Don't you believe that people can love again?'

'I don't believe they love with the same intensity.'

'That may be true, but most people need companionship; it isn't good to be alone.'

'To be alone isn't always to be lonely,' she murmured.

'You weren't born to be alone.' Seb pulled her close to him and yet again she submitted to him, allowing his kiss but not really feeling it. And sensing this he increased the force of his mouth on hers and bore her back against the cushions of the lounger. She felt in him a ruthlessness she had not suspected and with closed eyes she pretended he was Rique . . . Rique wanting her and hurting her with his desire.

'What a very cosy scene!' trilled a voice. 'Perhaps we shouldn't interrupt them——'

'Interrupt who?' This voice was male and demanding.

'Angie and your brother, my dear, locked in each other's arms under the orchid tree. Such a shame to spoil their fun!'

Angie froze in Seb's arms . . . his embrace slackened and he slowly turned his head to where Ysabel stood with Rique. Angie sat up and smoothed her hair and saw Ysabel's red mouth twist into a mocking smile. Nothing could have suited the other girl more; now she could go running to Don Carlos with the information that Angie had been caught red-handed playing around with his son Sebastian . . . it might be enough to get her dismissed from his household . . . sent away from Rique.

'There's no need, Rique, to look down your nose like that!' Seb climbed to his feet and stood facing his blind brother who had to imagine the scene . . . who couldn't do anything else but imagine that Angie had been a willing participant in what had taken place beneath the bauhinia tree.

'Don't go jumping to the wrong conclusions,' Seb went on. 'Angie and I are planning to be married.'

If at that moment a thunderbolt had fallen on Angie she couldn't have felt more stunned. She just sat there, hardly able to believe that Seb had said such an outrageous thing.

And then Ysabel laughed and spoke: 'Well, congratulations, you two!' She caught at Rique's arm and drew it to her side. 'Isn't that good news, *mio*? Let us hope your father gives his blessing on the match.'

Rique was staring at Seb as if he could see him. 'You haven't wasted much time, brother,' he said.

'Thanks to you. You've been the one who has made sure Angie and I have seen a good deal of each other since I came home. It's almost as if you planned for it to happen—did you, Rique?'

In the short silence that followed Angie felt almost stifled by the clamour of her heartbeats. Any minute now she was going to deny Seb's assertion, but first she had to hear Rique's reply . . . he had to deny that he wanted her to marry his brother.

'Very well,' Rique shrugged his shoulders and his lip twisted into the wry smile that was so much a part of him, 'I'll confess to a spot of matchmaking. Congratulations, Seb!'

'No!'

Angie felt sure she spoke the word aloud, but if she did Rique wasn't listening because he turned on his heel and suggested to Ysabel that they go and have some tea.

'Yes.' Ysabel held his arm. 'We'll leave the lovebirds to their own devices.'

Her laughter floated back to Angie, who had risen to her feet and was looking stormily at Seb.

'How dare you say what you said! How dare you do that?'

'You know Ysabel,' he rejoined. 'She'd have carried some sort of a tale to my father and put you in a shady light.'

'I know that, but I'd have dealt with it in my own way.' Angie could feel herself shaking. 'I have no intention of marrying you—you or anyone else—so you're going to have to tell Rique the truth!'

'I see.' Seb lunged for her wrist and caught it in a hurting grip. 'So it's my brother you are concerned about—I wonder why?'

'Because he's my patient, Seb. Because I don't want to be sent away from the Residencia until my work is done—I know how strict your father can be when it comes to a question of morals, but I feel sure I could have convinced him of the truth no matter what Ysabel implied. You took advantage of the situation——'

'So I did, *querida*, but people have to make things happen or they may never happen, so admittedly I used the situation to make you see reason. I want you, Angie——'

'Wanting is a two-way thing, Seb. Have you asked yourself if I want you?'

'You gave in to my kisses!'

'Because you were forcing me.'

'Be fair, Angie, you could have struggled a little harder than you did.'

'I didn't see the point,' she said coldly. 'A man usually gets the message when a woman doesn't respond.'

'And who has made you respond?' Suddenly his fingers were bruising her wrist and his dark eyes were glittering. 'It wouldn't be Rique, by any chance, would it? The opportunities are there when you're in and out of his bedroom at all hours of the night, soothing his hurt brow and playing his angel of mercy. Come on, I want to know—I demand it!'

'Let go of me!' She tried to wrench herself away from him, but his fingers were a shackle that wouldn't unlock. 'I—I never thought you could be like this—I thought you were kind——'

'I'm a man, Angie, and I don't feel very kind at this particular moment. I want to be told to my face that Rique means nothing to you as a man.'

'You're being hateful, Seb——'

'Tell me before I break your wrist!'

'That's nice talk!'

'I'm not nice right now. I want an answer to my question.'

'All right.' She flung back the hair from her brow. 'I mean nothing to Rique as a woman—does that satisfy you?'

'I suppose it must.' His grip slackened and he took a look at the marks he had made on her skin. 'No woman has ever driven me to cruelty before, Angie, so are you satisfied?'

'Oh, Seb,' she drew her wrist out of his fingers, 'now I don't feel that we're friends any more.'

'We aren't, *querida*. We are a man and a woman faced by a fundamental question, and it's this—will you allow it to be assumed that we are going to marry? I know what I want, but you seem like a girl going through some phase of hero-worship; you are nursing the brave warrior home from the battle and blind. What happens to you when Rique pronounces that he has no more need of you? Or worse still——'

'Please don't say it, Seb!' Angie felt the blood drain from her face.

'You crazy little fool!' Seb exclaimed. 'Rique couldn't have you if he wanted you—don't you know that? My father decided a long time ago that Ysabel was to come right into our family by marrying my brother, and that lack of sentimentality that made Rique a soldier will make it possible for him to enter into an arranged marriage. You saw them together just now—like unto like—as we are, though you refuse to admit it.'

Angie sighed. 'All the same, Seb——'

'Just try it on for size,' he murmured, and retrieving the wrist he had bruised he first kissed it, then slid on to it a slim gold bangle, the Spanish equivalent of the engagement ring. Angie felt the golden weight of it and realised that Seb had purchased it with the intention of proposing to her . . . and being accepted.

She lifted her gaze to his face and slowly ran her eyes over his Latin features . . . whatever had made her believe that Seb was less resolute than Rique?

'Please take it off,' she pleaded with him.

'If you want it off, *querida*, then remove it yourself.'

'We aren't playing a game——'

'I quite agree.'

'Then you meant all along——?'

'Yes. Tomorrow night at the patio party I meant to propose.'

'My answer, Seb, would still have been the same.'

'And my refusal of that answer would still have been the same. I can give you love, Angie—my brother can only give you a broken heart, one way or the other. He will marry Ysabel, don't you see that? He will do his duty by the family—he has been trained to obey the call of duty.'

Yes, she thought, and felt as if the blood ran out of

her heart and left her cold and chilled, though the sun lay like golden flame in the sky; the trees rustled in a breeze rising from the sea as dusk began to creep over the day.

'Do you feel cold?' Seb murmured.

She nodded.

'Then let me warm you, *cara*.' He took her back into his arms and she allowed him to do so. His body against hers felt warm and strong; a tang of cheroot smoke was on his clothes, and she felt a subtle need of his comfort, but it held not a flicker of the desire his blind brother could ignite within her.

A little later it was with a sense of surprise that she arrived back in her room adjoining Rique's to find that Seb's bracelet was still upon her arm.

She toyed with it . . . when Rique took her arm for guidance he would feel it there, and perhaps that was what she wanted now she knew that Ysabel was to be his bride and it was something his family had always known and accepted.

Oh lord, what was she to do? Angie sank down on her bed and rested her cheek against the cool footpost. Perhaps it might be best if she suggested to Don Carlos that she be replaced by another nurse . . . yes, perhaps after the party for Seb tomorrow evening she would see the Don and tell him that she wanted to return to England because she felt homesick. He was a kind and courteous man; he would understand.

She sighed, then tensed nervously as a hand fumbled at the handle of her bedroom door, hesitated, then pushed it open. Angie turned to look, half expecting to see Rique, but it was Maya standing there.

'Angie, I must talk with you!' She looked and sounded rather agitated.

'Then come in, Maya, and close the door.' Angie didn't know whether she felt relieved or disappointed that her visitor wasn't Rique.

His sister entered the room, an abstracted look on her face as she approached the bed. She wore a Spanish riding-habit, almost severely cut so that paradoxically it emphasised the feminine form. Maya's was in a light shade of brown, the skirt pleated, the shirt of cream silk, a Cordoban hat suspended from her wrist by a black ribbon; her kneeboots were of black leather. She looked extremely attractive, and Angie guessed that she had been out riding with Torcal.

'You look nice,' Angie smiled. 'Had a good ride?'

Maya nodded and sank down in the armchair beside the bed.

'You also look a little worried, *niña*. Want to tell me?'

Maya dug the heels of her boots into the carpet and studied her thoughts as if assembling them in some sort of order. 'How do we know when we're truly in love, Angie? I truly thought I loved that English boy, but I know now that it was just an infatuation, and in a way I was in rebellion against my father's Spanish ideas about women and their place in life. I've always been sheltered and chaperoned and so it was on the cards that I'd lose my head over someone . . . now I'm sure I've lost my heart.'

'Is it,' Angie hesitated, 'Torcal?'

The Spanish girl inclined her smooth dark head. 'You know, don't you, about what happened to Torcal? That's why you and Rique didn't want me to make friends with him—he sensed your feelings about him, so he carefully explained everything to me—are you surprised?'

'I'd have been surprised if he hadn't told you,' Angie said gently.

'He's such a dear—such a darling!' There was a catch in Maya's voice. 'I want to spend my life with him and I've told him so! I can't bear for him to leave Bayaltar without me—I just can't bear it, Angie! Oh, Angie, I expect you think me such a fool?'

'No.' Angie shook her head. 'He's a charming man, a man of integrity, and I quite understand your feelings. What are his feelings—has he told you?'

'He has told me that there can be no marriage between us.' Maya's eyes swam with tears. 'He insists that I shall forget him and fall in love with a young man who can love me and give me children—I don't want any other man! I want Torcal and I don't care—I don't mind—I want to live with him and make him happy, and I know in my heart I can!'

'You do realise, Maya, that apart from the question of children, you can never give him the very private and personal joys that a woman loves to give to the man she loves?' Angie moved her hands in a significant way, unaware in her concern for Maya that the lamplight relected in the sheen of Seb's bracelet. 'You know what I mean, don't you?'

Maya nodded and a teardrop fell to her cheek and slid down the smooth olive of her skin. 'I care so much about him that I would sooner be dead than not be with him—if I can't be with Torcal I shall take the veil! I mean it, Angie! I have told him so, and I shall tell my father so!'

'My dear, you must realise that Torcal sees all the pitfalls in a relationship in which compassion would have to take the place of passion. He's older than you, and some young man could come along and much as you care for Torcal, you might feel a physical response to someone else, and just think what that would do to such a man. Just think!'

'Angie,' Maya was staring at the golden bracelet on the slim extended wrist, 'are you in love?'

'Yes.' Angie's confession of love sprang from her heart a moment before her mind rang a warning bell . . . *Dios*, what had she said? Now Maya would ask for the man's name, and the man she couldn't name was Rique!

'Who?' Maya reached out and took hold of Angie's hand and admired the gold bracelet. 'Who gave you this?'

Angie groaned inwardly, for there was no evading the issue. 'Sebastian,' she said, and wished him on the other side of the moon for complicating her life in this way. 'But don't jump to any conclusions, Maya. In your brother's own words I'm trying it out for size, but that doesn't mean I intend to wear it for good.'

'It's very pretty.' Maya fingered the bracelet and looked wistful. 'If Torcal gave me a betrothal bracelet I should be delirious with joy, but I must say you look quite cool. Is it your English nature? Surely you wouldn't have allowed Seb to put the bracelet on your wrist if you didn't intend to marry him—you know it's our custom.'

'He rather took me by surprise.' Angie gave a wry smile. 'Both your brothers are self-willed and there are times when they refuse to take no for an answer. Just to please Seb I'll wear the bracelet for a day or two, then casually I shall return it.'

'Why return it?' Maya cocked her dark head. 'He's extremely handsome, don't you think? He's a very good catch, and you and he were always *simpatico* when we were kids. It would be nice to have you for a real sister, Angie—much nicer than having Ysabel!'

Angie's heart gave a painful thump. 'Is it true that she and Rique are expected to marry?'

'It's one of those arrangements.' Maya pulled a face. 'You know how I feel about her, but it's how Rique feels that counts.'

A silence enwrapped Angie in which love's agony seemed to tear at the vital centre of her. Seb's bracelet might have been black lead for all she cared . . . black, leaden like the weight of her heart.

'Do you think he—loves Ysabel?' she asked, and the words seemed to come from a distance, as though she stood away from them as if they were snakes that could strike at her. A strange, primitive feeling, awaking in her the awareness that love was primitive in people and in a way akin to the other basic things like war, famine, and the terrors of the dark. It belonged in that realm because it could hurt so cruelly.

It helped just a little that Maya shook her head. 'Often in Spanish families there is such an arrangement involving the eldest son.'

'But that seems so unfair,' Angie exclaimed. 'Supposing there was a girl he cared about for his own sake, would he set her on one side to satisfy the demands of family tradition?'

'Often in Spanish families it is done.' Maya heaved a sigh. 'Love is a hurting thing and it might be wiser not to fall in love, but it's part of living, isn't it, and when I look at Tia Francisca I realise how life can pass quickly taking the excitement of being young with it. I watch my aunt at her lacework and I see myself when I am her age, my life almost over and all my hopes and dreams gone quiet inside me. That's what will happen to me if I can't be with Torcal—don't you feel that way about my brother?'

Yes, Angie almost said, realising just in time that Maya meant her brother Seb. 'I like him enormously, but I don't love him.'

'You say it in a very certain way——' Then Maya caught her breath. 'I've just remembered what we talked about the other day—it's Rique you care for, and he belongs to Ysabel. Angie, we are a lovelorn pair, are we not?'

Angie had to smile at the way Maya said it. 'It would seem so, but perhaps it's for the best. At least we have the consolation of knowing that we care for men of honour.'

'I wish Torcal was the opposite,' Maya said moodily. 'I want so much to take care of him. I want to help him forget all the unhappy things he has gone through—the loss of his wife who was so young, and then being hurt in such a grievous way. I want to hold him in my arms until all the pain goes out of his eyes—is that what you would like to do for Rique?'

Angie nodded, and didn't mention that there had been nights when she had gone into Rique's room and found him tossing in a tormented sleep, lost in the dark and in need of a hand to guide him home through the realms of blackness where no lights shone for him.

More than once she had held Rique in her arms and soothed him into a more peaceful sleep and if he had

pressed his head to her breast it had been in the unaware way of a boy, almost, seeking comfort. If she
had gazed down at him with yearning eyes, there had
been no awareness of it in the blind eyes that gazed up
at her.

Ysabel would satisfy his physical hungers and enjoy
her position as the daughter-in-law of the Governor,
but she would never understand Rique's lonely fears,
nor his attacks of melancholy. Ysabel loved herself
more than she could ever love a man; Angie felt sure
of it.

All of a sudden Maya jumped to her feet. 'I'm not
going to submit meekly to what people say is good or
bad for me! I know Torcal needs me and I'm going to
Spain with him!'

Angie also got to her feet and gazed anxiously at her
friend. 'Are you quite wise, Maya, knowing all the circumstances as you do?'

'Would you be wise,' Maya retaliated, 'if Rique
wanted you?'

'No,' Angie had to admit.

'Then be on my side.' Maya's eyes were alight with
resolve. 'If Torcal won't take me with him, then I shall
follow him. I'm going to be his shadow until he admits
that we belong together. I want *him*, just as you would
want Rique even though he's blind. Love isn't a
demand, it's a giving, and if we're denied the right to
give, then we go cold and hard inside. You know I'm
right, don't you, Angie?'

'Yes.' Angie gripped Maya by the elbows and
studied her face for a long moment. 'When is Torcal
leaving the island?'

'He plans to go tomorrow evening, some time

during the party. A friend he has made at the hotel has his own launch and he's taking Torcal to Cordoba. I'm going to telephone Señor Maquinos at the hotel and ask if he'll take me on the launch as well; I shall ask him not to tell Torcal and say I want to surprise him. I shall leave the party with Torcal and plead that I want to wish him goodbye at the dock. He might make a fuss when I step on the launch, but he won't throw me overboard.'

Maya smiled. 'At least, I hope he won't. Angie, wish me God speed!'

Only moments later Angie was alone again; the door had closed eagerly behind Maya, who for good or ill had decided what she wanted and had found the courage to seek her fate.

'*Vaya con Dios,*' Angie whispered. '*Dios te proteja.*'

CHAPTER EIGHT

HER room faced the sunset and the windows seemed to glow like rubies. In the distance she heard the deep-toned bells of the Spanish chapel on the winding road above the sea. The bells and the brazen sky blended together and produced for Angie a sense of drama; a curtain-raiser to the evening that lay ahead, the *danza y musica* which was being held on the main patio of the Residencia.

All day the staff had been busy preparing the tables, hanging Chinese lanterns among the trees, and tapping casks of wine. Excitement tinged the air, for when a party was given by the Governor it was always a big one, with flamenco dancers and lots of good food.

The sun sank away and the golden glow died out of the sky. In a while the lanterns would be lit and guests would start to arrive, but Angie lingered in her party dress as her room darkened and almost concealed her slender figure there by the windows. Her dress was a jewel-blue silk, which she had shopped for that morning and been lucky enough to find in a shop along the Ramblas. Small opal-stoned earrings swung like tiny bells against her neck, and beneath the blue silk her figure had a delicate outline. She had applied some of her Chanel perfume and arranged her hair in a soft pageboy style.

Chanel, that amazing woman of fashion and the world, had stated that coquetry consisted in being shining clean. There was truth in the statement, Angie thought, for it always felt good to bathe and then slide one's speckless limbs into silky underwear. There was a sensuousness to it that made a woman feel as if she wanted a man to take her in his arms and breathe the perfumed cleanliness of her.

Angie was so lost in her reflections that she didn't realise there was someone else in her room until hands suddenly touched her, finding the silken curve of her hips.

'Don't jump like that.' The voice belonged to Rique. 'If I've startled you, then you must be standing in the dark.'

'I am.' His touch had set her heart racing though she stood very still, aware with every inch of her of his tall darkness and the warmth of his hands on her body.

'You feel and smell like a girl ready for a party.' His breath stirred her hair as he leaned down to breathe the scent on her skin. 'You told me, did you not, that my hands would become my sight and that my other senses would become more acute?'

'Yes, Rique.' Her own senses were acutely aroused by his nearness, and by the scented duskiness of the night beyond the windows. Music stole from the radio on her bedside table; a deep rich voice was singing an old song from a show, something about an enchanted evening and a stranger across a crowded room.

Rique would never be a stranger, but soon they would be apart across the crowded patio of his father's house, and some other girl would cling to his arm, dark hair piled high with a flower in it, the lantern light in her Spanish eyes.

'How delicately strange a woman feels when a man can only touch and cannot see her. What is the colour of the dress you're wearing, Angel?'

'Blue.' Her voice had a catch in it. 'Deep blue.'

'Blue is such an English colour, cool and distant like the sea and the sky. The night smells good as it drifts through the windows, "sea-foam and jasmine blowing . . ." I'm glad Seb has a fine night for his party . . . are you much in love with him?'

The question took her by the throat; when she was close to Rique there were no other people in the world. They were an intrusion she didn't want, least of all for him to bracket her with Seb.

'Do I trespass on hallowed ground?' He drew his hands from her waist and everything inside her ached for him not to retreat from her but to come closer still. 'I'll respect your reserve, Angel, but just let me say that you both have my wholehearted approval.'

Angie flinched from the words; they seemed to have razor edges to them that cut deep into her feelings. Then, because nature sought its defence when the body suffered, she found relief in a certain flippancy.

'I'm wearing Seb's bracelet right now, so I hope your father approves. Would you like to Braille it, Rique?'

'If you would like me to do so?'

She took his hand and fitted his fingers around her wrist so they could feel the smooth encirclement of his brother's bracelet, the Spanish equivalent of the slave shackle, she told herself cynically.

'Gold?' he murmured.

'What else?' Angie felt as if she were dying inside as Rique's fingertips touched the bare skin of her inner arm. 'All the harder to break, isn't it?'

'You want to marry Seb, don't you?' Now his fingers locked her wrist, making a double shackle.

'Like mad.' She felt brittle as breaking glass, right down to her knees that were actually trembling. 'He's so good-looking and doing so well for himself; what girl wouldn't feel that she has everything all tied up in one man? Weren't we always *simpatico*, Seb and I, and didn't you realise it in your infinite wisdom?'

'Angel, what is wrong?' Suddenly he had her by the shoulders and was swinging her to face him; now they were eye to eye in the dark, both of them lost in it for different reasons.

'Why should anything be wrong with me, *amigo*, when I have today become engaged to someone as charming as Seb?' Now she was in such an agony of love for this man who held her and yet gave her away that she would have said anything to protect her pride.

'Ysabel painted a very vivid picture for you, didn't she, Seb and I kissing madly under the orchid tree ... we can hardly wait to belong to each other. It's a fortunate thing, isn't it, that he isn't the eldest son and expected to marry a Spanish girl?'

'Is that what eldest sons do if they're Spanish?' A note of almost weary cynicism had crept into Rique's voice. 'I feel you trembling, Angel. Suppressed passion, I take it? We must arrange that you and my brother are married as soon as possible ... I wouldn't want to miss the nuptials.'

'Rique, for God's sake!' She pulled free of him and in doing so struck a shoulder against the window frame. 'Why must you harp on—dying? Is it what you want? I begin to wonder——'

'I know that I'm never going to see again,' he said sombrely. 'I forced Dr Romaldo to tell me that the optic nerves are damaged beyond repair. We are all human and we all live in hope of miracles.'

'The miracle, Rique, is that you survived, and you are physically resilient enough to go on surviving. The doctor must have told you that as well?'

Rique shrugged his shoulders and she caught the gleam of his ruffled shirt inside the dark material of his jacket. A slice of moon had appeared in the sky and was shafting milky light into the room; her eyes lifted to Rique's face and she saw the dark strength in it, the pride and power that would help him to fight the silent enemy inside his head; the waiting enemy with steel in its fist that sometimes jibed at him in the still dark hours of the night.

If only she were the one chosen to fight that enemy with him, but that right belonged to Ysabel, who would be impatient, or made afraid of the man who sometimes sweated with terror when he felt himself alone, and in pain, in his cage of black impenetrable bars.

'You are blind in more ways than one,' she exclaimed. 'Don't you feel your own strength ... can't you see that being blind hasn't diluted your courage?'

'You say that, Angel, but you have seen me thrashing about in fear——' He broke off and stared through the window, capturing the pale silver of the moon in his eyes. 'I have to admit that I shall miss your ministrations when Seb takes you away from the island, but I shan't, of course, stand in the way of love's young dream.'

Denial took Angie by the throat, the urge to cry out her heart to him was almost insupportable. She put a hand to her breast as if trying to press her heart in place ... her heart that was being pulled out of her by his lean litheness, the scars at his temple, the black eyebrows slanting like a devil's, the flared nostrils. Right here and now Angie realised that when a woman loved she no longer belonged to herself ... whether wanted or unwanted by the man concerned, a woman felt herself enchained to him by the very strength of her own feelings.

The radio played on, but the song had changed. *Liebesschmerz* in that deep rich voice. Love's agony!

'What sort of a night have we for the party?' Rique asked.

'Soft as sable,' she murmured. 'There's a crescent moon and the stars are shining over the sea.

'Then you should enjoy yourself tonight with your *novio*.' There was no mockery in his voice, instead there was a tinge of melancholy. 'The moon is said to excite women; a crescent moon, eh? The claw of the devil.'

'Rique——' Her hand found his sleeve and clung. 'I shan't leave you, *amigo*, until I know you don't need me any more.'

'That's magnanimous of you, Angel, but I suspect my brother's impatience to have you all to himself. I've learned quickly from you the things I need to survive in this cage of mine; you are free, my dear, to find your happiness with Seb. Now shall we go to the party?'

'Yes.' Her throat felt as if it had a band of iron around it and quickly she went across the room and switched off the radio . . . she needed music and wine and the numbing of the agony inside her; that song she didn't need right now!

'That was rather grand,' he said. 'German, wasn't it? I'm not well up on music; the songs that soldiers sing are usually rather naughty, and upon occasion outrageously sentimental.'

'*Liebesschmerz*,' she told him.

'Ah, something to do with love, I take it?'

'The agony of love.'

He stood silent a moment, while she watched him mutely, her hair luminous about her pale face in the moonglow.

'Tonight,' he said, 'you should be thinking of the rapture of love.'

She couldn't answer him, and he crooked his arm. 'Lead me to the fun and games, Angel. I need wine and song—flamenco song!'

'No women?' she murmured, as she took his arm.

'Only the beautiful Ysabel,' he drawled.

The lanterns outshone the moon and Angie was glad of it; the guitar music and the click of the castanets were so very Spanish that the lingering throb of *liebe* was held at bay, helped by the golden sherry which she shared with Seb. He, too, wore a crisply ruffled shirt but had removed his jacket, his dark trousers fitting close to his lean hips and long legs. He looked as Latin tonight as the young men who danced with the gipsy girls in their flamenco dresses, heavy with frills about their lissom bodies and bangled arms. Golden crescents hung from their earlobes, and there was hardly a woman at the party who hadn't a camellia or a carnation in her sleek dark hair.

Angie was an exception. She had pinned to her velvet purse the scarlet rose which Don Carlos had handed her. He then had kissed her hand and looked searchingly into her eyes. 'Sebastian tells me he wishes to be your husband, Angela? Is this so? Do you wish to be his wife, my child?'

Aware of Rique standing nearby with Ysabel, she had said yes . . . yes when her heart was crying out for him . . . him alone.

'Then this celebration is fortuitous.' Don Carlos had smiled graciously, but for just a moment his eyes had flicked to his tall blind son, the lantern light shining into eyes that couldn't see their enchantment, hung as they were among the trees and the trellised jasmine.

Angie, with her gaze upon the Don's face, had seen the pain in his dark eyes. There stood Rique, the first-born son who would never again see a woman smile or twirl her bright skirts as she danced to the flamenco music.

For most of the evening Seb kept Angie by his side, insisting that she eat slices of roasted pork and lamb, followed by strawberries and huge dark cherries.

She ate and drank; she smiled and conversed. She didn't miss the moment when Torcal said goodbye to Rique, and while they bade each other good luck and *adios*, Maya turned a moment to look meaningly across the patio at Angie. She was going with Torcal come what may, and Angie smiled and nodded and let it show in her eyes that she wished her friend all the luck in the world. She was setting out on a voyage that wouldn't be a smooth one, for love was rarely that kind of emotion. It was deep like the sea itself and as filled with risk as it was filled with rapture.

'*Dios te proteja*,' she whispered again in her heart. '*Vaya con Dios.*'

'You've gone very quiet, *cara*?' Seb touched her cheek, and then caught his breath as he felt moisture on his hand. 'What is it, my little one? What is wrong? Are you not enjoying the party?'

'It's a wonderful party,' she said huskily. 'I'm easily moved by music and the guitar can sound as sad as it can sound joyful.'

'For whom are you sad—Rique?'

'I suppose so.' She forced a smile and watched as a girl danced on a wooden table, swirling her skirts with a passionate delight in her own youth and all that it promised. Her eyes sparkled and beckoned, and suddenly a young man leapt to join her and there was a chorus of *Olé* from the people watching the performance.

The music quickened and throbbed and all around the patio the gaily dressed Spaniards stood absorbed in the age-old dance of love between a girl and a man. She eluded, he chased. She mocked, he grew angry. She smiled and thrummed the table with her heels while he circled her and went in for the capture.

During the applause Angie looked across the patio to where Rique was bending his tall head to Ysabel, listening to her as she languidly waved back and forth a beautiful fan of firebird feathers matching the colour of her dress. Her hair was dressed high and held with a Spanish comb in which was tucked a camellia. She looked exotic as a flower herself, Angie thought. Her Latin looks paid compliment to Rique's and to all outward appearances they were perfectly matched.

He raised his wine glass and that wry twist of a smile clung to his lips a moment before he swallowed wine and met Angie's gaze, almost as if he saw her. But he didn't see her. She was a black shape who held no meaning for him; for a woman to have meaning she had to be within reach of his hand . . . as Ysabel was.

'That was good, eh, the dance between those two?' Seb smiled down at her, handsome, his old kind self, admiring her with his dark eyes. 'You look so lovely tonight, Angie. The lanterns shine in your eyes—or do I still see tears?'

'Perhaps a little of both,' she confessed.

'You need a little more wine.' He took her glass. 'I'll go and fill up for both of us—stay just where you are, there where the jasmine tries to touch your hair. Look, it has spilled some of its petals on to you and you look like a bride.'

She watched him walk away, and then something

drew her attention back to Rique . . . some sixth sense that told her something was wrong. One of the gipsy dancers was tugging at his arm, pulling on him, laughing and urging him to come and show his footwork.

It was obvious she didn't realise he was blind, and in a sudden fury he dragged free of her. 'Go and find a man who can lead and who doesn't have to be led!'

With this he swung around, obviously with the intention of getting away from onlookers, and even as Angie cried out a warning he crashed straight into the hard trunk of a eucalyptus tree. There was a gasp of horror from those who had noticed, a suspension of the firebird fan so it stood in the air like a flame, and then Angie was running to him, to where he leaned dazed against the tree.

No longer did Angie care what anyone thought as she sped across the patio . . . only Rique mattered . . . poor dear Rique lost in the dark and cursing like a trooper.

'It's all right, my darling, I'm coming!' And then she was there and her arms were around him. 'I'm here!'

'Angel!'

'Are you all right, *amigo*?' She touched his forehead and felt blood on her fingers. 'Oh, you've hurt yourself!'

'It's nothing.' He held on to her and added tensely, 'Get me out of here, Angel. Get me away!'

Ysabel heard. 'What is this?' she demanded furiously. 'What kind of a spectacle do you think you're making of yourself—and Rique? Who do you think you are?'

'She's the only damn person in the world who

knows how I feel.' Rique sought Ysabel with his blind eyes, a trickle of blood running down from the graze on his brow. 'Is everybody looking at us? Has everybody seen what I do when I haven't got Angel to hold my hand? Seb, are you there?'

Seb was standing there with glasses of sherry in his hands and he was staring at Angie . . . Angie with her arms around his brother.

'I'm sorry, Seb,' she said contritely. 'I would never have married you—you knew it in your heart, didn't you?'

'I—suppose I did.' He lifted one of the glasses and drained it. 'So the tears were for Rique—is everything for Rique?'

She couldn't answer him, it was for Rique to say whether he wanted her or not; whether as nurse, guide or lover. It certainly had to be plain to everyone that he hadn't turned to Ysabel in his need. Ysabel was fluttering her fan with annoyance and looking at him as if his blindness was a nuisance to her rather than a tragedy for him.

'Seb.' Rique spoke with quiet command. 'Tell the musicians to play, ask the dancers to dance, and see that everyone goes on enjoying themselves. Where is Padre?'

'I think he had to go and answer the telephone— something to do with Maya.'

'Maya—isn't she here?'

'She went off with Torcal de Byas.'

'She has gone to Spain with him,' Angie said quietly. 'She knows all about him and she wants to be with him. She loves him.'

Rique heaved a sigh. 'Come, Angel, take me for a

walk. Take me to the beach and walk with me along the sands, and keep holding my hand—promise?'

'Oh yes!' Her eyes were shining. 'I should wash that graze for you and plaster it.'

'It won't kill me——' He broke off, then gave a short laugh. 'It will take more than that, won't it?'

'What about me?' Ysabel demanded. 'What do I do?'

'Find someone,' he said, 'who will tell you morning, noon and night that you're beautiful. Angel, shall we go?'

'To the moon,' she laughed, 'if you want to!'

Along the shaded, winding path to the beach the trees were giving off a dusky incense and fireflies lifted and fell inside the white trumpets of climbing vines. 'Here we are.' They stepped down on to the sand and they walked together towards the rippling surf. Sea and sky were smooth as satin, pinned together by the shining crescent of a moon. Everything was very lovely . . . a great sense of peace seemed to lie over the water.

'Is it very wonderful?' Rique murmured.

'Sheer Turner,' Angie told him, her arm tucked through his. She looked up at him and there were sparks of moon fire in his eyes; she waited, her heart pounding in her breast, for him to tell her what she must be to him.

'Strange how people talk softly at night, as if there are listeners,' he said. 'What are you thinking, Angel?'

'That the sea, the sky, the trees last so much longer than we do, and that it's so important to make the most of our lives.'

'So you knew that Maya was going to run away with Torcal?'

'Yes, she confided in me. She truly loves him, Rique.'

'And do you truly love me, *niña*?'

'Until the stars go out,' she said simply.

'They're out for me, child. They'll never come alight again, and if you take my hand I shall never let go of it again.'

'Here's my hand, Rique.' She tucked it into his. 'Oh, my dear, why did you push me away from you? Why did you do that to me?—you must have known how I felt about you. You must have guessed those nights I came to you and we talked until the dawn, until you fell asleep and I could tell you the daylight was coming.'

'Yes, but you're so young——'

'I'm a woman, Rique. Hold me close and you'll find out for yourself.'

Hard, strong and in need, his arms enfolded her and held her close to his heart. 'I'm not much of a bargain, Angel. Seb could give you a lot more than I can——'

'Then all right,' she pretended to pull away from Rique, 'I'll go and ask him to take me back. I'm still wearing his bracelet, you know.'

'Damn the thing—take it off this instant!'

She laughed and did so, tucking it into a pocket of his jacket.

'I'm going to give you one with a bell on it,' he said, 'then I shall always know where you are. Angel, kiss me!'

She locked her arms about his neck and put her lips softly against his. 'Rique, I love you so,' she whispered. 'I could never have married any man but you——'

'Proposing to me, *amada*?' He laughed and moulded her mouth to his. 'Do you really love your blind beggar?'

'Love is blind, isn't it, Rique? That's why people need each other—I need you, so much—so much!'

'Then abide with me, Angel—abide with me, my sweet young love.'

'It's all I want, Rique, all I've ever wanted.'

'Just for a moment assure me of something—did it mean anything when you kissed Seb?'

'He kissed me,' she corrected.

'You mean he made you submit to him?'

'Yes.'

'And the wearing of his bracelet?'

'A touch of defiance.' Her hand touched Rique's face tenderly. 'It was what you seemed to want, but I intended to give back the bracelet, and I even thought of going away from the island because it had become so painful, loving you and not—not being the one you loved.'

'I've loved you, *mi amor*, ever since you returned to the island; it grew out of the determined way you took me in hand and forced me, as you put it, to rejoin the human race.' He gave a slight laugh and held her locked to him. 'I still see you in my mind's eye as a kid with damp plaits coming undone from their ties, wet sand all the way up your legs. But when I touch you, then you become a woman I want as I have never wanted any other woman. My need, my Angel, is quite savage, but I think I could still let you go if you——'

'Don't say it, *querido*.' She pressed a hand to his lips. 'I'm not afraid to share your darkness; what I want is to light it up for you as much as I can. I've

loved you since I wore plaits and got sand up my legs.
I always longed to belong to you—quite simply,
Rique, I'm yours—yours to do with, *señor*, as you
will.'

'Mine,' he said, with a soft exultance. 'My eyes—my
soul!'

The sea rippled and the moon sailed high. Angie
leaned there against Rique's shoulder and sighed with
happiness. She had come home to Bayaltar to stay, and
it would be for Rique to tell his father the Governor
that an English girl was going to be his bride.

Somehow she didn't think that Don Carlos would
be too unhappy about having her in the family.

Harlequin understands...

the way you feel about love

Harlequin novels are stories of people in love—people like you—and all are beautiful romances, set in exotic faraway places.

 Harlequin Books

Available at your favorite store or from Harlequin Reader Service.

In the U.S.A.
1440 South Priest Drive
Tempe, AZ 85281

In Canada:
649 Ontario St.,
Stratford, Ontario N5A 6W2

What readers say about Harlequin romance fiction...

"You're #1."

"Thank you for the many hours of lovely enjoyment you have given me."

"The books are so good that I have to read them all the way through before being able to go to sleep at night."

"Thanks for many happy hours."

"Harlequin books are the doorway to pleasure."

"They are quality books—down-to-earth reading! Don't ever quit!"

"A pleasant escape from the pressures of this world."

"Keep them coming! They are still the best books."

Harlequin Presents...

The books that let you escape
into the wonderful world of romance!
Trips to exotic places…interesting
plots…meeting memorable people…
the excitement of love….These are
integral parts of Harlequin Presents—
the heartwarming novels read by
women everywhere.

Many early issues are now available.
Choose from this great selection!

Choose from this great selection of exciting Harlequin Presents editions

Relive a great romance...
with Harlequin Presents

Complete and mail this coupon today!

Harlequin Reader Service

In the U.S.A.
1440 South Priest Drive
Tempe, AZ 85281

In Canada
649 Ontario Street
Stratford, Ontario N5A 6W2

Please send me the following Harlequin Presents novels. I am enclosing my check or money order for $1.50 for each novel ordered, plus 75¢ to cover postage and handling.

☐ 99	☐ 103	☐ 109
☐ 100	☐ 106	☐ 110
☐ 101	☐ 107	☐ 111
☐ 102	☐ 108	☐ 112

Number of novels checked @ $1.50 each = $ _____

N.Y. and Ariz. residents add appropriate sales tax. $ _____

Postage and handling $ _____ .75

TOTAL $ _____

I enclose _____
(Please send check or money order. We cannot be responsible for cash sent through the mail.)

Prices subject to change without notice.

NAME _____
(Please Print)

ADDRESS _____

CITY _____

STATE/PROV. _____

ZIP/POSTAL CODE _____

Offer Expires February 28, 1982.   106563170